Enrollment Form

☐ **Yes!** I WANT TO BE A **P**RIVILEGED **W**OMAN.

Enclosed is one *PAGES & PRIVILEGES*™ Proof of Purchase from any Harlequin or Silhouette book currently for sale in stores (Proofs of Purchase are found on the back pages of books) and the store cash register receipt. Please enroll me in *PAGES & PRIVILEGES*™. Send my Welcome Kit and FREE Gifts -- and activate my FREE benefits -- immediately.

More great gifts and benefits to come like these luxurious Truly Lace and L'Effleur gift baskets.

NAME (please print)

ADDRESS   **APT. NO**

CITY   **STATE**   **ZIP/POSTAL CODE**

PROOF OF PURCHASE SAMPLE ONLY

Please allow 6-8 weeks for delivery. Quantities are limited. We reserve the right to substitute items. Enroll before October 31, 1995 and receive one full year of benefits.

NO CLUB! NO COMMITMENT!

Just one purchase brings you great **Free Gifts** and **Benefits!**

(More details in back of this book.)

Name of store where this book was purchased_____

Date of purchase_____

Type of store:

☐ Bookstore   ☐ Supermarket   ☐ Drugstore

☐ Dept. or discount store (e.g. K-Mart or Walmart)

☐ Other (specify)_____

Which Harlequin or Silhouette series do you usually read?

_____

Complete and mail with one Proof of Purchase and store receipt to:

U.S.: *PAGES & PRIVILEGES*™, P.O. Box 1960, Danbury, CT 06813-1960

Canada: *PAGES & PRIVILEGES*™, 49-6A The Donway West, P.O. 813, North York, ON M3C 2E8   **PRINTED IN U.S.A**

Dear Reader,

Do *you* have a secret fantasy? Everybody does. Maybe it's to be rich and famous and beautiful. Or to start a no-strings affair with a sexy mysterious stranger. Or to have a sizzling second chance with a former sweetheart.... You'll find these dreams—and much more—in Temptation's exciting new yearlong promotion, Secret Fantasies.

Always tantalizing and provocative, Tiffany White has written another sensation in *Naughty By Night*. Her heroine, Ashleigh Frost, lives out what many women wonder about. Ashleigh turns herself into the ultimate sex object...but then the threats begin. And the action heats up when Detective Cade Hawkins arrives on the scene.

In the coming months, look for Secret Fantasies books by Janice Kaiser, Mallory Rush and JoAnn Ross. Please write and let us know how you enjoy the "fantasy."

Happy Reading!

The Editors
c/o Harlequin Temptation
225 Duncan Mill Road,
Don Mills, Ontario M3B 3K9

Dear Reader,

When my editor suggested I'd be perfect for the Secret Fantasies miniseries, I was thrilled. If you've read any of my previous books you'll know I have a penchant for fantasy.

I grew up poor, which meant I dreamed a lot. I can remember seeing the pretty little blond girl wearing shiny black patent leather shoes, pristine white gloves, a velvet headband and a frilly party dress and wondering what it would be like to be her.

Then there was my first trip to the bakery. The front window was lettered with shiny gold script so I knew something wonderful was inside. When I opened the door a tiny bell tinkled and heavenly smells wafted out to tantalize. All the treats were presented on lacy paper doilies. What would it be like to eat one of each?

I can recall the first time I visited the library in an English estate house. Leather furniture, a big fireplace, walls of leather-bound books, thick carpet and dark wood. What would it be like to curl up there and read whatever I wanted?

And then there was the first song I heard on the pulsating neon jukebox. Rock and roll—so naughty and so appealing.

Is it any wonder that I now curl up in a leather chair in the library with a bluesy saxophone wailing on the CD player, wearing Victoria's Secret secrets beneath my jogging suit, munching on black licorice jelly beans as the images of ultimate bad boys like Rhett Butler, Brad Pitt and Jack Nicholson whisper wicked ideas into my ready ear?

I hope you enjoy *Naughty By Night*. Like the heroine, I've always wanted to drive a roomful of men crazy—though I can usually do it just by opening my opinionated mouth. I love hearing from my readers. Please write.

Tiffany White

"Come here often, do you?"

Ashleigh tried not to show how happy she was to see Cade again at the diner.

He took a chair without asking and sat there grinning. No, she realized, it was half smirk, half grin and all innuendo mixed with a dollop of invitation. To what, she didn't have to guess. Cade Hawkins was made for women.

She slipped a bite of her cobbler into her mouth, making it look like the best thing she'd ever tasted—other than him.

"That's not very hospitable, you know," he said, looking longingly at the dessert.

"Funny, I don't recall inviting you to—"

"Sugarpie, you've been inviting all kinds of things...."

Ashleigh gave in and fed him a piece of her cobbler. A speck of whipped cream sat on the corner of his lip.

She felt her tongue search out the very place on her own mouth.

Cade smiled wickedly and flicked the speck of whipped cream from his lip with his forefinger and offered it to her. *But she knew he was offering so much more....*

When asked to describe her life, **Tiffany White**
told us that in her fantasies she flies to the coast
for weekend visits with friends, sees all the latest
movies, fills her closets with the newest fashions
and regularly wins the *Romantic Times* Most
Sensual Author Award. In reality, Tiffany dresses
in sweatshirts and leggings in her office when she
writes, travels home to veg out with videos and
has become the Susan Lucci of the coveted
Romantic Times award.

Books by Tiffany White

HARLEQUIN TEMPTATION

367—FORBIDDEN FANTASY
407—A DARK AND STORMY KNIGHT
442—BAD ATTITUDE
465—NAUGHTY TALK
490—LOVE, ME
514—A KISS IN THE DARK

Don't miss any of our special offers. Write to us at the
following address for information on our newest releases.

Harlequin Reader Service
U.S.: 3010 Walden Ave., P.O. Box 1325, Buffalo, NY 14269
Canadian: P.O. Box 609, Fort Erie, Ont. L2A 5X3

Tiffany White
NAUGHTY BY NIGHT

Harlequin Books

TORONTO • NEW YORK • LONDON
AMSTERDAM • PARIS • SYDNEY • HAMBURG
STOCKHOLM • ATHENS • TOKYO • MILAN
MADRID • WARSAW • BUDAPEST • AUCKLAND

For Tiffany Nicole Brumitt
who looks excellent in white.

Thanks to Wendy Haley who likes
to see a good man sweat.

ISBN 0-373-25650-7

NAUGHTY BY NIGHT

Copyright © 1995 by Anna Eberhardt.

This edition published by arrangement with Harlequin Books S.A.

® and TM are trademarks of the publisher. Trademarks indicated with
® are registered in the United States Patent and Trademark Office, the
Canadian Trade Marks Office and in other countries.

Printed in U.S.A.

Prologue

POLICE DETECTIVE Cade Hawkins had his buzz haircut and hotshot attitude long before Keanu Reeves sported both in *Speed*.

When the guys at the station began calling him Speed, he let his hair grow. The attitude, however, remained.

"What were you thinking?" Captain Gavin bellowed, the top of his bald head turning pink as he swiveled around in his desk chair to face Cade when he entered the office.

"I, ah, guess I wasn't thinking," Cade admitted, looking back through the glass top of the partition to see if the guys were watching him being chewed out. They were, grinning.

"Not with anything above the waist, you weren't," his captain agreed. "You're thirty years old, not some rookie."

It was common knowledge at the police station that Cade Hawkins had never met a woman he didn't want to rescue.

But this time he'd picked the wrong woman.

Big time.

His captain wasn't done with him. "It's bad enough that you went to bed with the attorney defending a cop killer, but then you let her get you on tape saying the cop was a wife abuser, that he'd nearly killed her. Your lady love took that information to the judge's chambers to get the case dismissed—"

"Damn it, Captain, you know I didn't know I was being taped." Cade unfolded his swimmer's body and pretended sudden interest in George Washington's portrait on the wall. The portrait was as old as the rest of the battle-scarred furniture in the police station.

"Let me guess . . . You were too busy—"

Turning, Cade interrupted his boss's tirade. "I promise not to do it again," he said, raising two fingers in a Boy-Scout pledge because he knew it would annoy Gavin.

"Damned straight. Just to make sure, I'm sending you to Vice to give you some time to think about it."

Cade couldn't believe it. "Vice!"

"Vice. They've got a special little detail just for you."

"Give me a break, Captain. It's not like Anderson wasn't a dirty cop. Every cop in the department knew he beat the shit out of his old lady every time he felt like it just because she'd say hello to a guy. Anderson's wife deserved to get off on self-defense, because that's what it was."

"I've heard that before—*on tape*. What the devil is wrong with you? You were a witness for the prosecution. What you did is called 'sleeping with the enemy.'"

There was no use arguing further with the captain. Cade knew when his boss had his mind made up. Better to allow him to cool off, and then maybe . . .

Scowling, he left Gavin's office, berating himself for being a fool. Why was he such an idiot where women were concerned? He didn't regret getting Mrs. Anderson off; only "sleeping with the enemy," as his captain had put it. He was old enough to know better. He envied his partner, J.J., who was happily married. Love eluded Cade, so he settled for sex, which never did.

A few minutes later he was on his way out of the police station, brushing past Melodie Fortune, the attorney who'd burned him, on her way in to see a client.

She grabbed his arm. "I hope you aren't upset with me, Cade. It was just business."

He pulled his arm free and kept walking.

Easy for her to say.

She wasn't the one busted to Vice.

1

"IF YOU WEREN'T SUCH a romantic son of a bitch, you wouldn't be in this position," Cade Hawkins muttered to himself as he tossed the basketball into the air. It sailed over the hoop and slammed with a jarring rattle against the backboard. Bouncing off it, the ball missed the basket completely. Cade swore.

Dribbling the ball on the paved surface of the park court, he played alone in the early morning. His black tank top and shorts were soaking wet. He'd been trying to work off the frustration he felt at being transferred to Vice. He was a homicide cop, damn it. Not some bluenose interested in policing other people's morals.

He squinted his green eyes to avoid the sweat dripping from his midnight-black hair.

"Help! Please, somebody—help me!"

Cade was off in a flash, running in the direction of the woman's scream.

At this hour the park was almost deserted. Sizing up the situation with his cop's eye, Cade saw he was the lone person responding to the woman's scream.

He kicked off his sneakers as the distraught young woman on the wooden bridge spanning the pond pointed in desperation to the small boy flailing wildly in the water several yards away from her.

"Please, help me! My son can't— I can't swim! He's drowning—hurry!" she cried, her eyes wide with fear.

Cade was way ahead of her, diving into the pond, scattering the flock of squawking ducks the two must have been feeding. Just as he reached for the child, the boy disappeared underwater.

"Michael—n-o-o-o!"

The young mother's frantic scream fueled Cade's already pumping adrenaline and he lunged beneath the surface for the child. Grasping the boy's shirt, he pulled him up and swam to the bridge, where he handed the child up to his mother.

The mother sobbed hysterically over the small limp body while Cade hauled himself up onto the bridge. Instantly wresting her son from her, he began CPR. Within seconds the boy coughed up water and started crying.

Cade slumped back, letting the mother comfort her child while he caught his breath.

The woman's eyes mirrored her thanks. "You saved my son's life. How can I ever repay you?"

"Promise me that when you get home, you'll sign up for CPR classes and both of you will take swimming lessons."

The young woman nodded as her little boy's cries settled into whimpers.

"Are you going to be all right?" Cade asked, rising and helping her to her feet.

"Yes, we'll be fine . . . thanks to you."

Cade lifted the little boy's chin. "And you, young man, you almost got nibbled by the ducks."

His comment got a shy smile from the little boy.

Cade's mood had improved considerably when he left the two of them to go and retrieve his basketball. After picking up the ball, he headed back to his Jeep. The big black German shepherd in the passenger seat lifted its head from its paws, his tail wagging in welcome. Shadow was a police-academy flunk-out, and Cade's best friend. Cade had named him Shadow because the dog was afraid of his own shadow.

Stowing the basketball in the back seat, Cade climbed into the Jeep, patting Shadow's head.

IT WAS CRUEL FOR the loan officer of First National Trust to keep her waiting in his mauve-and-gray office for over a half hour, Ashleigh thought. But then everything about the bank was sleek and cold, even the ugly fish mounted on a plaque on the wall behind the banker's desk.

She had tried every bank in town for a loan—to no avail. Even if her pride had let her ask her parents, retired and living on a fixed income, they couldn't help her.

"Here I am, again trying to gain someone's approval," she muttered under her breath. An only child, Ashleigh had been born to her parents late in life. Afraid they would spoil their daughter, they continually withheld their approval. Ashleigh had tried to follow her mother's dream that she become a ballerina, only to have that hope dashed by a last growth spurt when she was eighteen that resulted in "totally inappropriate" curves.

At twenty she'd tried to please her parents by marrying the older man they had handpicked for her.

That had been another failure when the marriage lasted only a year; a failure that had brought her to First National Trust—and to her knees.

She just had to get this loan. With it she could get her life on track. A life that at twenty-one she had never been in charge of. Without the money, she didn't know what would become of her.

She was no longer her parents' sheltered child.

She was no longer her husband's shy bride.

She was on her own. And scared. And angry.

The door to the office finally opened and the loan officer joined her, a folder of paperwork in his hand that he laid on his desk before him when he took his seat in the gray tweed executive chair.

The portly sandy-haired banker looked over his glasses at her and said, "You've run up quite a debt, young lady."

"No," she countered, trying to keep her desperation from her voice. "My husband did. He was a compulsive gambler. A year into our marriage I found he'd completely destroyed our credit along with running up the debt. When he refused to get help, I divorced him. He's since disappeared and the creditors want me to repay the debt."

"The debt is in both your names," the banker reminded her, shaking his head. "I'm afraid you're a bad credit risk. However, if you were to remarry, it might well improve your rating—"

"You're saying you won't approve the loan," she said through clenched teeth.

He nodded.

"I'm sure it won't be difficult for an attractive young woman like yourself—" gray eyes as cold as those of the dead fish on the wall appraised her dancer's body approvingly "—won't have any problem finding—"

Ashleigh was out of her chair and out of the door of his office before he could finish.

She bolted from the bank, too angry to see. No way was she going to let anyone else control her. For the first time in her life she was going to do what she wanted. She was going to stop seeking approval from others, find a way to retire the debt her ex-husband had saddled her with and then pursue a career in fashion design.

Her husband had only pretended to support her dream of becoming a fashion designer, calling the classes she took at the local college a "hobby."

It was not a hobby. She would have a career. One that *she* chose.

Ashleigh spent the next couple of hours wandering in Shaw Park.

As she watched a couple swinging a toddler on a swing set in the sand, an idea began forming in her mind, a sort of contingency plan. It was an idea she hadn't allowed herself to really consider before, but now she had no other option.

By the time she'd walked from the swings and sandbox to the tennis courts, she'd reached a decision.

Miss Olivia's was her only option.

The two guys lobbing tennis balls back and forth probably went to Miss Olivia's, she thought, noting their expensive tennis togs. The tony strip club had opened a new franchise in the neighborhood, a fashionable cosmopolitan suburb in Clayton,

Missouri. Its very existence had caused a burst of opposition, with the local restaurants losing business to it stirring the controversy. While some women's fantasies might run to driving a roomful of men crazy with lust, Ashleigh's fantasies ran more along the lines of flashing haughtily in front of her ex-husband and a dozen or so bankers.

She was a good dancer and knew she could make a lot of money very quickly, working at Miss Olivia's. It might even be good therapy as well as a way to repay the debt; she would be taking her clothes off and essentially saying, *Look, but don't touch*. The same thing her ex-husband had said about her desire for a career, the same thing the smug bankers had said about their damn money.

She knew she could do it.

She could.

For a moment the years of polite "shoulds" she'd let rule her life assaulted her, causing doubts. It was hard to go against her natural need to please others, not to care what everyone thought.

But she banished any second thoughts.

She was desperate. She would do whatever she had to do to take back her life.

She would.

"YOU CALL THAT punishment? I should be so lucky," said Jerome Johnson, the big, dark-eyed muscular cop who'd been in Cade's academy graduating class. He made no effort to try to hide his lack of sympathy for Cade's plight. "I wish the department would punish me by assigning me to hang out at a strip joint."

"You even think of going near Miss Olivia's Finishing School for Young Ladies, J.J., and your Monica will finish *you*," Cade retorted, laughing at his friend who had one of the few happy cop marriages on the force.

"You got that right," J.J. agreed, taking off his jacket as the two of them got ready to run laps at the gym.

"Nice jacket," Cade observed, needling him.

Monica was a fashion buyer and forever bringing home "finds" for J.J. to wear. As a result he was the best-dressed cop on the force—a fact that no one would let him forget.

J.J. gave Cade a dirty look. "Maybe someone will steal it," he said hopefully, shooting Cade's worn jean jacket a covetous look.

"Not unless you pay them money to do it." Cade hung up his jacket and changed into running clothes. The two of them headed for the track to work off calories and job frustrations.

"Nice T-shirt," J.J. said, noting they both wore the same one advertising The Dry Dock, a jock/

cop bar they frequented for Monday-night football. "What's the deal at the strip club, anyway?"

"The mayor's leaning on the chief to close down the place and my assignment is to find a good reason to do just that. Seems the local restaurants don't like the competition and are leaning on the mayor, crying moral outrage."

Their feet slapped the track floor in a synchronized rhythm as the two fell in step at a brisk pace. "Well, you've got to admit a strip club is hardly fair competition or going to be popular with the chamber of commerce in an elite community that wants to be known for its culture."

"Miss Olivia's is hardly your average strip club."

"Aren't you being a bit defensive?"

"No. Miss Olivia's is a franchise. It's as upscale as the gourmet restaurants that are objecting to it."

"So then you've been to one before...." J.J.'s dark eyes twinkled.

They rounded another lap, and Cade let J.J.'s teasing banter slide. "I do my homework," was all he said. "How's the Kerrigan case going?"

"Don't ask. The captain is steamed because some of the evidence seems to have sprouted legs and walked out of the evidence room. We may not have enough to go to trial, and you can imagine how thrilled the captain is to have that spotlight on his department once again."

"Don't remind me. Looks like we're both in the doghouse," Cade said, his breathing showing the effect of the laps they'd run.

"I like your doghouse better than mine. The captain ain't that pretty to look at. At least you get to ogle pretty women and call it work."

"I'm not looking at any women. I'm not talking to any—"

"Right," J.J. interrupted Cade's vows of reformed behavior. "First one of them with a sob story and you'll be—"

"No, I won't. I've learned my lesson. I want back in Homicide, not a transfer to Traffic. I'm going in and find a reason to close down the place. I'm not looking to the right or to the left. I'm doing the job and nothing more. I'm not getting involved."

J.J. got tickled and started laughing so hard he had to stop running. He stood bent over with his hands resting on his knees as he got back his breath.

"What's so funny?" Cade demanded.

"Last time I heard you making vows like that, you ended up bringing home Shadow."

"Shut up, J.J."

"Don't say I didn't warn you," J.J. countered, going into a spree of laughter at the face Cade made.

ASHLEIGH TOOK A SEAT at a vacant table near the back of Miss Olivia's and ordered a glass of white wine to build up her courage to ask for a job.

While she waited for her drink, she checked out the decor of the club. It was done in Art Deco style. All the tables, decorative moldings and other furnishings were made of black lacquer. The walls were covered in a mauve-and-blue geometric design and hung with sensual prints in the same colors. The club looked fashionable and expensive, right down to the oversize potted greenery.

At least she wasn't the only woman in the place with her clothes on, she noticed, continuing to glance around the room.

While it was true most of the tables were occupied by men in groups or alone, there were also several tables of couples. That fact gave her hope. The club couldn't be that bad if women felt comfortable being here.

On the small stage located at the front of the room a young woman danced to a popular country song about cowboys. Gyrating to the high-energy music, she was gradually removing her skimpy Western-style outfit. By the time her number was over, the pretty girl was down to cowboy boots, fringed G-string and two strategically placed stars.

It did not escape Ashleigh's notice that the stage gave the young woman a degree of protection from the customers. Other than the performer no one was allowed on it. There was no tucking of folded bills into her costume nor any physical contact with the customers whatsoever. In fact, the waiters were all so well-built, they looked like they doubled as bouncers.

That the performer she'd just seen wasn't all that great a dancer bolstered Ashleigh's confidence enough for her to ask the waiter if she might see the manager.

"You aren't a cop, are you?"

"No. No, of course not," she assured him, all serious fluster until she saw that he'd been teasing.

The waiter surveyed her and nodded to himself. "You're here about a job."

"What makes you say that?" All of a sudden she was affronted.

"Two things. You've got a great body... and you're very nervous."

"Oh." She supposed she couldn't really take offense. Everything he'd said was on target.

"As it happens you're in luck. Cassie is quitting to go back to school. I'll tell the boss you want to see him."

Ashleigh swallowed the last of her wine as she waited, not wanting to think what her interview would be like. She had never actually interviewed for a job before, had never had a job. And now she was—

"Hello, you wanted to see the manager?"

Ashleigh looked up at a tall middle-aged man with no hair on his head and lots on his face.

"May I?" He indicated an empty chair at her table.

She nodded, feeling her face flush. Surely he wasn't going to interview her at the table within earshot of some of the customers.

"I'm the manager, Tommy Gardner."

Ashleigh took his proffered hand. She thought it telling that he'd said "Tommy" instead of "Tom." He probably loved his job; only a certain kind of man didn't drop the *y* from their name as they became men. The kind who never grew up. What better place for him to manage than Miss Olivia's?

"The waiter said you might be hiring a replacement dancer," she began, unable to get the word *stripper* past her lips.

"That's true enough. One of our best girls is quitting to go back to school to get her master's. She financed it at Miss Olivia's. Have you ever danced before— I'm sorry, I didn't get your name."

"Ashleigh. Ashleigh Frost. I've been in dance class since I could walk," she assured him.

"But have you ever danced in front of an audience before. It takes a—"

"Of course, I've danced before an audience," she said, full of impatience. "I was studying to be a prima ballerina."

"Last time I was at the ballet, they kept their tutus on, I believe."

"Oh. Oh, you mean have I ever 'danced' before? Well . . . no." Her voice cracked and she rushed to cover it. "But I don't think it would be . . . I mean, I think I can. . . ."

He gave her the same once-over the waiter had.

"Tell you what. I'm in a bind so I'll try you out. Go back and find Cassie. Tell her I said she should loan you one of her costumes and we'll see what the customers think."

Ashleigh felt her throat tighten as she swallowed dryly. "You mean now? Right now? In front of . . ." She tilted her head.

"It's up to you, if you want a chance at the job. The crowd is thinning out. It won't be so bad. Just remember to smile."

Smile. Like anyone was going to look at her face. No, she couldn't think like that. If she did, she wouldn't be able to do this, and she had to. Right now, it was her only shot at coming out of the mess she'd gotten herself into.

"Okay," she agreed and pushed back her chair.

"It's down the hall and on your right," he directed, staying at the table to wait.

It took all her determination not to bolt. She wasn't prepared. It was something she'd thought she'd have time to work herself up to.

The Art Deco design of the club extended behind the scenes as well, Ashleigh noted, as she tried to find Cassie. There was a huge mural picturing voluptuous women on the wall of the blue-and-mauve painted corridor.

She knocked on the first door she came to that looked likely.

"Go away," came through the door to startle her. The voice was husky and self-assured.

Just as Ashleigh was turning to do just that, the door swung open.

"Who are you?" the tiny blonde with the big voice asked, studying her.

"Ah, Mr. Gardner sent me back to see—"

"Oh, Tommy sent you. Okay, come on in. What are you—a reporter or something? You'd think he'd tell me so I could at least be presentable, wouldn't you?" she said, pulling on a robe. "I guess the first thing you want to know is how much money I make. That question always comes even before what am I doing here...."

Ashleigh did want to know, but didn't stoop to pretense to get the information. If she passed her impromptu audition, she'd know the going wage soon enough. And if not, well, she would only be depressed to know what she'd missed out on.

"No, Cassie, you don't understand. I'm not—"

"I'm not Cassie."

"Oh, dear—" Ashleigh fidgeted with her hands "—I'm sorry. Mr. Gardner said to find Cassie and ask her to lend me one of her costumes so I could audition for a job as a dancer."

"So you're not a reporter," the petite blonde said, pausing in her primping. "I thought since you looked so serious and everything... You don't look like a dancer—well, a ballerina maybe, but not a strip—"

"I was a ballerina," Ashleigh interjected to keep her from saying the word. "But I sort of outgrew it."

"You sure did. I'd lend you a costume myself, but you've got more legs than I've got body. Cassie is already gone, but I'm sure we can find one of her costumes that'd fit you. Come on, her dressing room is across the hall. My name is Cathy. The girls call me Chatty Cathy 'cause I never shut up."

"Ashleigh."

"Pretty name. You're really nervous. I can tell by the way your hands are shaking," Cathy said, opening the door to Cassie's dressing room. "Let's see what we can find you."

"Are you sure Cassie won't mind?"

"Naw. Cassie's great. I'm going to miss her. She let me borrow all her romance novels. It gets pretty boring in between, waiting to go on."

"I never thought about that." Ashleigh watched as Cathy flipped through the half-dozen costumes hanging in Cassie's closet. She pulled one out and held it up for Ashleigh's approval. "What do you think?"

"Superwoman?"

"It's got a cape for you to hide behind." Cathy whipped the red cape across Ashleigh's body, draping her.

"I'll take it."

Cathy handed it over. "You need any help getting ready?"

"No, I'll manage somehow. How much time do I have?" she asked, eyeing the abbreviated costume. It was a long way from a dying swan to Superwoman.

Cathy tilted her head and listened to the music. "Darla's on now, so you've got about ten minutes. I'll come back and knock when it's your turn. And don't worry—everybody's nervous the first time." Cathy left, pulling the door closed behind her.

Left alone, Ashleigh took her costume off the hanger and made quick work of getting dressed. She knew if she gave herself time to think about it she might lose her nerve. Especially if she thought about how beautiful the other dancers were. She felt quite plain by comparison. Her dancing would have to sell her.

She was standing in front of the mirror giving herself a pep talk and trying not to feel ridiculous in the red cape, boots and blue-and-gold star-spangled costume, when Cathy knocked, calling out, "Your turn, Ashleigh."

Ashleigh opened the door and took a deep breath, then followed Cathy to the stage entrance.

The music started and Cathy gave Ashleigh a little shove propelling her onto the stage. Unable to move, she stared at the audience. Mr. Gardner had been right; the crowd had thinned out. There were maybe twelve people left. A group of four guys near the stage looked up, waiting expectantly. Their ties were loose and they had the relaxed look of employees whose boss was out of town.

A couple sat, engrossed in each other.

The rest of the tables were occupied by men who showed varying degrees of interest. The guy at the end of the bar didn't even glance up.

Mr. Gardner nodded for her to start her performance. Closing her eyes for a moment, she let the music take over and then began.

Executing a turn while swaying her body, she hesitated, then began peeling off one of the Superwoman cuff bracelets. It stuck and taking it off required so much concentration she messed up a pivot and almost lost her balance.

A chuckle drifted over from the end of the bar. So the guy was watching, after all.

Finally she got the damned bracelet off and just barely kept herself from flinging it at the dark-haired man who'd laughed. She restrained herself only because he'd probably think it was a sign of favor; he was good-looking enough to have just that sort of ego.

Concentrating on her dancing, remembering it was her only ace, Ashleigh moved to the beat of the music. She didn't perform any grinds, just classic dance moves—dressed in the strapless Super-woman leotard.

After working free the other bracelet, she worried about what to remove next. She glanced over at Mr. Gardner and he pointed to his lips. Smile. She was supposed to smile.

She pasted a smile on her face and bent to slip off the soft leather boots that were only a half size too big. She and Cassie were apparently off on cup size, as well. The top of the costume threatened to spill her out to the enthralled foursome up front. Straightening quickly, she removed the other boot by bracing her foot against the wall.

Her smile faded; she was running out of costume.

She stalled by dancing some more. A waitress brought the guy at the end of the bar a drink and took an order for another round from the four men up front.

The stall was over then and it was time for the taboo, the forbidden. Either she took off the rest of her costume or she didn't. Once she did, there was no going back. She would have crossed over a line in her mind.

She thought about the debt, her ex-husband, the bankers. Although she wasn't smiling, she reached behind her back and slowly began unzipping the back of her costume beneath the red cape. The cape should have been discarded already, but she wasn't ready to abandon the safety of it just yet.

That was a good thing—

Because when her costume slipped to the floor and she stepped away from it, two gold stars fluttered to land at her feet. Either the glue hadn't worked or she hadn't applied them correctly. Whichever, it gave the alluring image of her being completely naked under the silky red cape that hugged her curves in an intimate caress.

She could see desire glinting in the eyes of the four giddy men up front. And it gave her a rush of power—an unfamiliar feeling.

She liked it a lot. Liked the self-confidence it gave her. Unbidden, a smile came to her lips.

The music suddenly ended and she left the stage.

Backstage, Cathy hugged her. "See? I told you that you could do it."

"Well, I didn't exactly 'do' it."

"Close enough. Everyone has to get up their nerve to get comfortable onstage. You're such a good dancer, though, that Mr. Gardner is sure to hire you on the spot."

"Do you really think so?" Ashleigh pushed open the door to Cassie's dressing room.

"I do. Well, I've got to run. I've a dentist's appointment that I need to get to. You know how Mr. Gardner is about having a perfect smile."

Ashleigh laughed at the face Cathy made and waved her off.

Ten minutes later she was dressed and standing in front of the club manager, anxious for the verdict on her future.

"We'll give it a try. You're going to have to work to get better, you know. But your dancing was great and your smile wasn't half bad. Cassie is leaving in a week. That will give you time to work on a costume and your act."

"Thank you, Mr. Gardner," she said, as the waiter waved him over to the phone.

The review from the guy at the end of the bar when she passed him wasn't as good: "Honey, you suck. You ought to look for another job."

Ashleigh wouldn't meet his eyes; instead she brushed past him, hurrying from the club so he wouldn't see the tears his words had provoked.

So he couldn't see that she cared what he thought.

2

THE DRY DOCK BAR had four TVs over the long polished-wood bar that stretched the length of the main room. Each of them was tuned in to ABC's Monday-night football game. The Dallas Cowboys were playing the Arizona Cardinals and beating them as usual. The game wasn't holding anyone's attention any more than the posters of scantily clad women on the wood-paneled walls.

A lively game of pool was going on in the back room.

Detectives Allen and Brown were regaling J.J. and Cade with a lurid tale of a sting operation they'd been involved in.

"So, how's it going with your cushy new assignment, Hawkins?" Allen taunted, his blue eyes twinkling. "Had to arrest any naked ladies so far?"

"Yeah, bet it's pretty hard not to get distracted when you're putting handcuffs on a naked woman, huh?" Brown elbowed Allen and they both broke up. The curly-haired cousins were always ready to rib a fellow cop.

"You two are just jealous. Don't pay them any mind, Cade," J.J. said.

"Hey, we're not the ones responsible for letting the antique dueling pistol walk away from the evidence room just so we could try to get reassigned to be on Cade's cushy gig. Did that evidence ever turn up? Man, I haven't seen the captain that steamed since someone put the condom in his wallet for his wife to find," Allen said.

"No, the murder weapon hasn't turned up," J.J. answered glumly. "Don't the two of you have to be somewhere?"

"As a matter of fact we do," Brown replied, checking his watch. "Come on, Allen, we've got to find the serial bank robber before he gets a nervous trigger finger. He's made a clean getaway from four broad-daylight robberies."

"Well, here's a big clue for you," Cade said, getting even. "He's not a vampire."

J.J. and Cade high-five'd each other as Allen and Brown groaned and moved off.

"Hey, you want to stop running off business," the Tom Selleck look-alike bartender called out as he watched the two detectives leave.

"Just getting rid of some troublemakers, Dave," J.J. assured him. "Send someone pretty over here with a beer."

Dave brought the beer himself.

"I said someone pretty," J.J. reminded.

"You're married, and this one—" he nodded at Cade "—needs to stay out of trouble for a while. Though, how he's going to do that spending all his time watching women take off their clothes is beyond me."

"Does *everybody* know?" Cade asked J.J.

"No. I'm sure someone in the city has been out of town and not checked their messages."

"I don't suppose it would do any good to tell you all I'm innocent, that I've been framed."

"That's usually the perp's claim, not the cop's, Cade."

"Well, it's true."

"Well, don't tell anybody or they'll have you back in Homicide looking at dead bodies instead of at Miss Olivia's looking at lively naked ones."

"Homicide is where I belong," Cade insisted.

"I think I'll watch the game," Dave said, getting up, his eyes glazing over at the cop shoptalk.

The bar erupted in cheers as the Cardinals missed an extra point, and J.J. and Cade's attention was drawn to the game on TV momentarily.

"That's a new shirt, isn't it, J.J.? What would you call that color exactly?" Cade asked, tongue in cheek.

"Mulberry. And it's silk, okay? I tried telling Monica that real cops don't wear silk, but—"

"Yeah, women just don't listen, do they?"

"Oh, they listen, and then they do what they want anyway."

"You mean we do what they want anyway."

"Yeah, that too.

"Hey, Dave, how 'bout some chili over here?" J.J. called out, his stomach reminding him he hadn't eaten since the granola bar for breakfast. "So, how's it going, Cade? You don't seem to have gone blind or anything yet from watching women take off their clothes."

"That isn't what makes you go blind, J.J.," Cade said dryly, taking a swig of beer.

Dave brought two bowls of chili over and a bottle of Tabasco sauce. "It's a new recipe my sister Doris tried out. Let me know what you think."

Cade and J.J. dug into the chili and concentrated on the game on TV. The Cardinals were making an attempt at a comeback. A half hour later the comeback hadn't materialized and the Cowboys had scored another touchdown. The two friends gave the chili a thumbs-up to Dave when he came to collect their empty bowls, then returned to more interesting conversation.

"So, Cade, been sleeping with any more attorneys lately?" J.J. teased.

"Perish the thought. I've sworn off professional women."

"How about the girls at Miss Olivia's?"

"I told you I'm not looking, or talking to any of them."

"Uh-huh."

"J.J.—"

"Come on, Cade, there has to be at least one girl you've noticed. . . ."

"They're all alike. You've seen one, you've seen them all. The novelty of nudity wears off real quick. There's only one who—"

"Aha! See, I knew it," J.J. interrupted, tipping his beer to his lips, a gleam of satisfaction in his eyes.

"You need to get Monica to stop traveling so much, J.J. I'm not having adventures for your neglected libido. This girl wasn't even any good. I told her she needed to find a new job."

J.J.'s grin was just short of a laugh. "My libido's just fine. Every time Monica comes home, it's like our honeymoon. Now, tell me this girl's story— she's stripping to support her sick grandma, right? I know there has to be a sob story. You'll be getting involved and bringing her home before you know it."

"Not a chance. She was auditioning. No one in their right mind would have hired her. She couldn't even keep her pasties on."

"*Pasties?*"

"Miss Olivia's is a high-class club."

"Doesn't sound like you're finding much to please the captain, so far."

"If there's something there, I'll find it."

"But what if there isn't anything there?"

"I don't even want to think about that."

"Well, keep me posted on the girl, anyway," J.J. said.

"There is no girl."

ASHLEIGH SAT on the hardwood floor of her bedroom in her pastel pink dance leotard, white tights and pink ballet slippers. She'd been flipping through a stack of fashion magazines since she'd finished her daily dance regimen an hour ago. Things weren't going well.

She needed to make a costume, but the problem was she didn't know what kind of costume because she didn't know what her act was going to be. Inspiration hadn't struck her as she'd hoped it would.

The fact that she had a chance at the job at all still surprised her after the pitiful performance at her audition. Performing had been much harder than she'd expected. It wasn't the club; it was classy. It wasn't the customers; they were respectful. It was her own problem with her body.

She'd been in denial about it so long that she might as well have been in a convent. All the years when she was planning to be a ballerina, she'd starved herself to fit the image. And had been successful. But when her growth spurt hit, womanly curves destroyed all her hard work. She hadn't faced her anger. She'd simply given up. And when her parents had coaxed her into marriage because she wasn't trained for any other career than ballet, she'd gone along with it, swallowing her anger. And when her husband had preferred being out at night alone to their marriage bed, she'd meekly accepted the situation.

Now both her spirit and her body were making struggling attempts at independent expression.

Both had been angered by the bad "review" given by the good-looking stranger at the end of the bar.

She'd vowed that she would show him.

And that she'd show herself.

Dancing at Miss Olivia's wasn't going to be her life's career, but it was going to help her get it. She was determined not only to make enough money to pay off her debt as quickly as possible, but to be the best performer at the club.

She kept flipping through the pages of the magazine, hoping she'd get inspired by an outfit she could copy that would work for her—something unique.

Oddly enough, it was an article that gave her the idea—an article about men's fantasies.

Restacking the magazines, she went to take a shower, and think through her idea. She always got the best results thinking in the shower.

By the time she was finished showering, she had the complete act worked out in her mind. She began sketching her costume.

Either her act would be a smash hit, or an utter failure, she knew. Silently she wished for the former.

At any rate, she'd eliminated the need to figure out how to make those dumb stars stay stuck when she danced—she wasn't going to use any.

CADE FELT A WARM BREATH on his cheek and he heard panting. He opened one eye to see a pair of soulful brown eyes staring at him.

"Go away," Cade said, rolling over and punching his pillow.

A pitiful whine was followed by a paw tugging at his forearm.

"Shadow, it is entirely too early in the morning to get up and go outside to play Frisbee. We'll wake the neighbors. We've been over this before. We don't get up around here until the sun comes up. You're a dog, not a rooster, pal, okay?"

Shadow lay beside Cade with his head cocked to one side as if he were not only listening, but understanding every word his master said.

Cade knew it was all an act.

Shadow and Cade both knew that Shadow could get his way anytime he wanted. Cade was a pushover because he felt guilty about the amount of time he had to leave Shadow alone.

Cade squeezed his eyes shut, bent on sleep.

Shadow whined again and then pulled out all the stops, licking Cade's ear.

"Oh, for heaven's sake, Shadow, don't you have any pride at all?" Cade shoved back the covers and reached for the clothes he'd worn the day before: jeans, sneakers and a Dry Dock T-shirt. He picked up the Frisbee, the soft kind that wouldn't hurt the dog's mouth when he caught it, and headed for the hallway.

But Shadow didn't follow.

Cade called him, but he didn't come.

Cade traipsed back to the bedroom to where Shadow lay on the bed, his head resting on his paws.

"What is it, boy? Did you hear a noise and you want me to check the house for bad guys again?"

Shadow just lay there, looking up at him with his big brown eyes.

And then a streak of lightning flashed, followed by a growling roll of thunder.

"So that's what's bothering you, boy. You heard the storm coming."

Shadow thumped his tail against the bed and Cade came to pet him as rain suddenly began to fall, making a fierce racket against the skylights.

"It's okay, boy. It's only a little thundershower. When it's over, we'll go out and play Frisbee."

Shadow wasn't convinced. At the next loud crack of thunder, the dog plowed under the covers to hide out the storm.

Cade shook his head at the cowardly lump under the covers. He wished it was that easy to solve life's problems. If it was, he'd join Shadow.

His week hadn't gone well at all.

He hadn't been able to find a good reason to close down Miss Olivia's. And worse, he didn't think he was going to.

Oh, well, at least that girl had taken his advice and not come back.

3

ASHLEIGH SAT in Cassie's old dressing room, which was now hers. Decorated in mauve and black, it had a print sofa and chair, half-size refrigerator, well-lit black lacquer dressing table, and an ailing potted palm.

The costume she'd designed and made hung neatly in the closet while she did a few leg stretches to warm up for her performance. When she'd arrived, Mr. Gardner had given her employment forms to fill out and told her what her probationary salary would be. The generous amount would increase considerably if he was happy with her performance today.

Finishing her exercises, she searched her purse for a pen and began filling out the forms to keep her mind off what she was about to do. She was only somewhat successful. She was still nervous when she'd completed the paperwork and set it aside to get ready.

Ten minutes later, it was her turn to perform.

She hung her robe on a coatrack off to the side of the stage. Then, taking a deep breath, she walked onstage.

All her years of ballet training showed in her perfect carriage and graceful control. When she reached the center of the stage, she stood very still as if she were a statue.

A murmur went up from the crowd.

They had noticed two things. The first was the lack of music. The room was very quiet. As she continued to stand center stage, a smile formed on her lips; she'd succeeded in gaining the crowd's full attention.

Even *his*.

Her critic was back. Six feet of dark hair, green eyes and disapproval.

Only this time, he wasn't seated at the end of the bar, but at a table up front near the stage. She felt her nerves quiet as she took the challenge in his eyes. No way was she going to let him brush off her performance like he had before. He would remember her act. Everyone would.

She knew the nude bodysuit she'd designed to fit her like a glove made her look stark-naked. She'd purposely designed it that way. But she also knew the crowd had been taken by surprise; wondering what she was doing . . . wondering why she was starting out with nothing to take off.

Ashleigh bent forward from her waist and her long dark hair tumbled forward to brush the floor. Slipping the plastic-coated rubber band from her wrist, she gathered her hair into a ponytail and straightened, giving the crowd its first clue of what she planned.

Picking up a soft white ball from the chair to her left, Ashleigh lowered her body to a sitting position and unrolled a pair of pristine white anklets. Keeping her long legs straight, she again bent from the waist and, one by one, slipped her feet into the anklets, showing off her ballerina's flexibility.

She folded the sock cuffs around her trim ankles, then leaned back on her elbows to admire her handiwork. Lifting her legs ever so slowly into the air, she began kicking them, scissorslike. The white anklets were a flirty accent to her prettily arched feet.

Ashleigh then turned on her side, resting her head in her hand, and stared straight at *him*. Holding his green eyes captive, she slowly bent one knee and then raised her leg perpendicular to the floor. In her mind everyone in the crowd receded except him. She had an audience of one.

And she held him captive.

Next she added a pair of white sneakers.

The short white pleated skirt she stepped into ended high on her thighs. The blue sweater she pulled on came to just above her waist. It had a large white letter *C* that settled on her breasts.

Her outfit was as abbreviated as a Dallas Cowboys cheerleader's. More so.

Everyone in the audience remembered that she hadn't put on panties. The nude bodysuit she wore reminded that she was "naked" under the brief pleated skirt—a mental image that was refreshed when she started doing cartwheels around the stage; slow, sensual, perfectly executed cartwheels.

When her round of cartwheels was finished, she did a couple of high jumps, as if her team were winning—and judging by the hushed, attentive crowd, it was.

Moving off to the side, she picked up two blue-and-white pom-poms and returned center stage.

She raised one pom-pom above her head and called out, "Give me an *A*."

The crowd was silent, caught off guard.

A tall blond guy at a table in the back caught on when she waited and called out, "*A*."

That was all the encouragement Ashleigh needed.

"Give me an *S*," she continued, her voice firmer.

The audience responded.

She went through the spelling of her name. "What does it spell?" she called out when she was through.

"Ashleigh," was the enthusiastic response.

"What does it spell?" she called out again, putting her cupped hand to her ear and looking at Mr. Gardner's smiling face.

"Ashleigh!" came the shouted response, louder than before.

She smiled, satisfied she'd accomplished her goal. Everyone was paying attention.

Even *him*.

Catching and holding his green eyes again, she executed the climax of her act, scissoring her legs apart and sliding ever lower until her body caressed the floor in a perfect split.

When she saw him swallow dryly, she straight-armed a pom-pom above her head in a sign of victory.

As she left the stage to a round of thunderous applause she heard the buzz of conversation begin about her performance. Cathy was waiting off-stage and pulled her into a hug.

"That was great. And so different. Where did you get the idea? Will you help me with my act?"

"Your act is terrific as it is. Everyone loves you, Cathy."

"You think so?" Cathy was obviously in the line of work for the attention it brought her.

"Of course. How could they not? You'd better go get ready, you're on soon." Ashleigh went back to her dressing room to change.

Sitting there alone, Ashleigh considered her performance. It had gone better than she'd dreamed it would. Her worries about being hired were gone. In their place were new concerns.

She'd applied for the job because of the money it paid. Her sole focus was to pay off the debt she owed and get on with her life; to lift the constant worry from her mind, to stop the collectors from calling her.

Applying for this job would never have occurred to her under any less dire circumstances. It wasn't that she herself had any quarrel with a place like Miss Olivia's; she hadn't in fact thought about it one way or the other.

What she had to deal with now was the fact that she had gotten a tremendous amount of pleasure out of performing. It had made her feel very sexy. And that was a new feeling for her. She was a little bit embarrassed by it. Had she been harboring another side of herself—a wanton hussy just dying to get out?

She didn't think so, not really.

When she thought about it, what had made her feel sexy wasn't performing for a crowd, but performing for *him*.

Who was he?

Why did he hang out at Miss Olivia's?

Maybe Cathy knew.

Ashleigh dressed in her street clothes and went out to watch Cathy and give Mr. Gardner the employment forms she'd completed.

After she'd dropped off the papers to her boss and he'd responded with a thumbs-up on her performance, she was stopped by the blond guy who'd given her an *A*.

"Could I buy you a drink?" he asked.

"No, thank you," she said, and started to move away.

"Well, then, could you answer a few questions for me. Mr. Gardner said it was okay."

"He did?"

The man nodded. "I'm Harry Wolfe, a reporter for the River City *Call* and I'm doing a piece on Miss Olivia's."

He pulled out a chair and Ashleigh sat down nervously.

Signaling the waiter for a refill, he sat across from her, watching Jennifer with the long black waist-length hair begin her performance from the corner of his eye.

Ashleigh would bet this was a job the reporter was going to make last as long as he could; it was obviously an assignment that was right up his voyeuristic alley.

"What do you think about the controversy?" he asked, taking out a notepad.

"Controversy?"

"Yeah, you know. About the restaurants around here all being in a panic about the business Miss Olivia's is luring away from them."

"I don't know anything about it."

"How long have you been working here?"

"I just started."

"Really? That's some act you've got there."

She was beginning to feel uncomfortable, thinking that maybe sitting down with the reporter hadn't been such a good idea. Harry Wolfe wasn't just wanting to report on the controversy over a strip club in the middle of a posh business district; he wanted to feed it. He wanted her to say something that he could run with. Cathy came by the table to say goodbye and Ashleigh introduced her. Chatty Cathy happily took over the interview and Ashleigh made an excuse to leave.

It was chilly out and she pulled her wrap around her as she walked the several blocks to the coffee shop across the street from the Clayton court-house and the police station. The irony of the police station being so close to Miss Olivia's wasn't lost on her. The coffee shop did a steady business with all the attorneys, cops and dancers.

The place was busy as she slid into a booth. Someone had left a newspaper lying on the table. Pushing it aside, she gave the teenage waitress her order for a cup of coffee.

"Wise move. There's never any good news to read in the paper, anyway," said a masculine voice. "Mind if I join you for a cup of coffee?"

She wondered if "green eyes" had followed her from the club—and couldn't deny feeling a certain sense of pleasure at the idea.

"Why?" she asked.

"I'm thirsty. . . ?" He glanced around the packed room, obviously recognizing most of the customers. "And there isn't a free table."

She shrugged, trying not to betray her interest.

"So your name is Ashleigh. . . ." he said, taking a seat across from her in the booth.

"What do you want? Did you follow me here to give me another bad review?"

There was a ghost of a smile on his lips and his green eyes glinted. "If I did, I'd be lying. You know how good you were.

"Why?" he asked when she didn't comment.

"Why what?" she demanded, taking her cup of coffee from the waitress.

"Why didn't you take my advice and find another job?" he said, nodding to the waitress's inquiry if he wanted coffee.

"Who *are* you?"

"Just someone who can see that you don't belong working at Miss Olivia's."

She took a sip of coffee. "And where is it you think I belong, as if it was any of your business...?" He was great looking and arrogant; even she knew that was a dangerous combination—an appealingly dangerous combination.

"I don't know. On some rich man's arm, maybe. Someplace safe."

"Been there, done that," she countered, annoyed. Look where it had gotten her.

"What'd you do? Run through all the poor fool's money and then dump him?"

"He dumped me," she replied, taking perverse pleasure in batting his assumptions back in his lap.

"Oh. Well, there must be something other than work at Miss Olivia's you can do."

"You sure seem to have mixed ethics. You hang out there, yet you keep trying to discourage me from working there. What are you? A preacher or something?"

"No." He ran his hands through his dark hair and she read frustration in his green eyes. It was like there was something he wanted to tell her, but for whatever reason he couldn't. "You think this is just a temporary job, don't you?"

"What if I do?" She couldn't believe she was even having this conversation with him. Why didn't she just get up and leave? She'd vowed no man was going to tell her what to do, and here she was, listening to this stranger.

"You're wrong. You'll get caught up in the rush you get from the power. It will wind up controlling you."

"What are you talking about?"

"Easy money. I've seen it before, seen what it does to good people."

"I'm not quitting."

The waitress brought his coffee.

He put two spoonfuls of sugar in it. Sweetening he really needed, as far as she was concerned. He stirred his cup of coffee reflectively.

"Then maybe you can help me."

"Do what?" she asked suspiciously, peering at him over the rim of her coffee cup.

"Nothing much. Just keep your eyes and ears open to what's going on at Miss Olivia's. If you see or hear anything that disturbs you, I want you to tell me about it."

"Why are you so interested in what goes on at Miss Olivia's?"

He tapped his spoon on the side of his cup and laid it on the table. "I'm conducting an investigation. I can't tell you anything more than that."

"Can you tell me your name?"

"Oh, sorry, Cade Hawkins," he said, extending his hand.

She took it and felt a surge of appreciation for his masculinity. His hand was big, his grip powerful, yet gentle. This was a man on whose arm she'd feel safe.

But she wasn't looking for "safe." She was looking for independence. She pulled her hand away.

Cade finished the last of his coffee and rose to go. "See you around," he promised, then turned to leave. He took a few steps, stopped and glanced back over his shoulder. "Nursing is a good career. You might want to think about being a nurse."

After he'd left she did find herself thinking about nursing. About a little white cap . . . white stockings . . .

She could hardly wait to see Cade's face.

WHEN ASHLEIGH ARRIVED at Miss Olivia's the following day, Cathy stopped her on her way to her dressing room.

"Have you seen this?" Cathy asked, handing her the newspaper she'd brought to the club with her.

"What is it?" Ashleigh scanned the headline, expecting to find what Cathy meant there.

"No, check the entertainment section. Harry Wolfe mentions you in his column."

"He does?" Ashleigh paged through the newspaper until she found his column and scanned it.

"The club ought to be packed today after the rave review he gave your performance. Of course, Mr. Gardner isn't going to like the overall tone of the column. He won't be pleased about the controversy."

"Don't kid yourself, Cathy. Controversy brings in customers. I wouldn't be surprised if Mr. Gardner weren't stirring things up behind the scenes just to get the publicity. He's the one who probably called Harry Wolfe and not the restaurant owners."

"Gee, I never thought of that."

"Men can be very devious. They'll do what they have to to get what they want."

"That's pretty jaded, Ashleigh. Some men may be like that, but they aren't all. There are some good men."

"How old are you—nine?"

"You're just a cynic."

"No, I'm right."

"So, you're saying never trust a man? *Any* man?"

"Right." Especially one with dark hair, green eyes and wonderful hands. One who wouldn't tell her much more than to trust him.

She handed the newspaper back to Cathy, but Cathy refused it. "You keep it for your scrapbook. I've got to go see what Mr. Gardner wants."

Ashleigh took the newspaper even though she didn't have a scrapbook or any remote intention of getting one; Miss Olivia's was just temporary—a means to an end.

She went into her dressing room to hang up her costume and mentally prepare herself to do the job that was going to bring her independence.

But she didn't hang up her costume. Instead it slipped from her hand to the floor when she saw the mirror over her makeup table. A message was scrawled there in bright-red lipstick.

GET OUT!

4

As Ashleigh sat on a stone bench in Shaw Park, she looked up from her sketch pad to watch a little boy and a poodle puppy chase after a red balloon that had escaped the child's grasp. The poodle caught the balloon first, its sharp claws bursting it with a loud pop.

The little boy's lips puckered, but before he could cry his mother scooped him up and diverted him with the promise of ice cream—ice cream that the puppy would no doubt get when it fell from the cone.

Ashleigh's attention returned to her sketch and she began thinking about the warning left on her dressing-room mirror the night before.

At first it had frightened her.

And to be honest, it still unnerved her.

But she wasn't going to let it stop her. She wasn't going to "get out." No one was going to tell her what to do for whatever reason.

Certainly not a jealous co-worker, if that's what this was all about. She found it hard to believe that any of the girls she'd been introduced to so far by Cathy would mean her serious harm.

Trisha with her long dark hair and Midwestern accent had good reason, as she'd been set to be the star.

Pamela was as bouncy as her shag brunette haircut and smiled all the time as she had in her cowgirl number when Ashleigh had come to apply for the job.

Cathy had been nothing but helpful and kind to her from the start.

The twin redheads, Mitsy and Bitsy, only worked weekends.

Those and a few assorted new girls who were trying out weren't going to intimidate her.

And she was discovering that she wasn't just a good little girl. She was a woman, with a woman's desires surfacing.

Working at Miss Olivia's was going to have a secondary benefit she hadn't anticipated. It would allow her to work through who she was as a woman, to explore her sexuality.

She wasn't going to listen to Cade Hawkins, the mystery man who wanted her to quit.

He thought he knew what was best for her.

Who was he, anyway? she wondered. Why did he hang around Miss Olivia's? He was great looking. It wasn't as if he needed to pay to watch a woman undress. All he'd have to do was ask and most women would be glad to oblige.

He'd said he was conducting some type of investigation. But he purposely hadn't said who or what he was investigating.

Had one of the local restaurant owners hired him to find some way to close down Miss Olivia's? Or maybe he was working for a wife who was worried her husband was straying.

Or maybe he was lying.

All she had to recommend him was what she could see with her eyes; not a half-bad recommendation, but one that had more to do with lust than anything else.

She'd forgotten to ask Cathy about him. The newspaper reporter, Harry Wolfe, had thrown her off course with his search for a comment he could use to fuel the fire of controversy between Miss Olivia's and the restaurants that were claiming moral outrage at the club's very existence in their "nice" neighborhood.

Finished with her sketch, if not her questions, Ashleigh left the park to purchase the fabric she would need to make a new costume. She'd decided against the nurse's outfit because it would have given Cade an advantage—knowing she'd paid attention to what he said.

"SO HOW'S IT GOING?" J.J. asked, as he ran around the track with Cade.

"It's not. I can't find anything illegal going down at Miss Olivia's."

"And the woman?"

"What woman?"

J.J. shot him a look. "Come on, Cade. This is me you're talking to. The woman you talked into quitting stripping. Have you 'called on her' yet?"

"She didn't quit."

"But I thought you said—"

"Yeah, well, I was wrong. She's back. She replaced a dancer named Cassie."

"So you got double trouble, then," J.J. observed, nodding to Detectives Allen and Brown, who'd waved up at them as the pair entered the gym on the lower level below the running track.

Cade continued looking down at his feet, scowling. He didn't notice the two detectives' arrival. His mind was on the jam he found himself in. "No, I don't have double trouble. I've still only got one problem. The same one I've had since the captain put me on this rinky-dink detail in Vice. I've got to find a way to close down Miss Olivia's to make the captain happy so he can make the chief happy so he can make the mayor happy so he can make the restaurant owners happy—you know the food chain. That's the only way I'm going to get back into Homicide where I belong. Working Vice is thankless."

"I see," J.J. said, not believing his buddy's words for a moment. Cade might find a reason to close down the strip club, but there was no doubt in J.J.'s mind that Cade would also find a way to get Cassie's replacement another job. Cade just couldn't help rescuing women. Must be something in his DNA. Monica said it was just that Cade was one of the last nice guys—after him, of course—and that J.J. wasn't to get any ideas about rescuing women.

"This woman you aren't going to rescue, what's her name?"

"Ashleigh. That's spelled *A-s-h-l-e-i-g-h.*"

"I thought—"

"She spells out her name in her act," Cade explained.

"I won't ask. Listen, when we're done here, you want to go play some pool?" J.J. asked, as they started their final lap.

"Sorry, pal, I promised Shadow some Frisbee in the park. I'll catch you next time."

THAT EVENING CADE fought his way past the chain of picketers outside Miss Olivia's. A pale thin guy with a dark goatee was clearly the instigator, his shouted speech bringing a chorus of agreement from the other picketers. Cade recognized the man as the owner of the restaurant a block away that bore his name, Vincent's. Vincent Palmer was a snob of the first order and if he had his way there wouldn't even be a restaurant around that didn't have escargots on the menu. Certainly not a strip club that served food.

Once inside Miss Olivia's, Cade had to share a table with a stranger. The place was packed. It appeared to be date night with a mostly mixed crowd. The single guy he shared a table with looked like he'd walked out of a Ralph Lauren ad. Cade was surprised to see him alone as he looked very datable. Of course, Cade was alone, too, and he supposed some similar suppositions were being made about him.

"Name's Dexter Murry," the blond, brown-eyed six-foot preppie offered, extending his hand to Cade when the cowgirl stripper finished her act.

"Cade Hawkins."

"Boy Tommy is raking in some money. I'd like to have a percentage of what this joint is making. It's about time we got some entertainment around here. It's not like everyone wants to go to the symphony and ballet. There *are* some real men left."

Cade just nodded, glancing about the room to see if there was another table open that he'd missed on his first look around. There wasn't. He was stuck with motormouth and his love affair with the sound of his own voice. Great, just great. He just loved working Vice.

A waitress came with Cade's designer water that he let ol' Dex think was a cocktail. Cade tipped her well.

The music started up again and a cute blonde announced as Cathy came out. Her act was done to the latest Aerosmith song, which, given any of their music videos, was custom made for stripping.

Cathy had a friendly kind of sexiness. As she began taking off her clothes she invited the audience to begin clapping, seeming to gain encouragement from their approval.

"She's got a great body, don't ya think?" Dexter commented, watching the blonde shake it provocatively.

She did. But Cade wasn't the sort of guy who discussed such things with total strangers. So he let Dexter's question pass unanswered. Instead he gave the menu a quick glance and waved the waitress over to take his order for a T-bone steak and baked potato—then added an order of nachos and cheese for an hors d'oeuvre to share with Dexter as a means of shutting him up.

"Look how limber she is. Doesn't that get you really hot?" Dexter went on, commenting on the blonde's slow backbend to a handstand.

"She must have a gymnastic background," Cade said, turning his attention back to the stage and the girl who was trying so hard to win attention.

"She does. She was junior state champion in the all-around event. She can pick up—"

"You know all that from watching her?" Cade interrupted, not wanting to hear where Dexter was going with his description of Cathy's talents.

Cade was shocked more by Dexter's reply than by the finale to Cathy's act. "Naw, I know everything about Cathy because she's my wife."

"Oh."

The order of nachos smothered in melted cheddar cheese came just in time.

Dexter was busy munching through the next act: a girl with waist-length black hair that she wrapped around her like a lover. Dexter seemed pleased that the applause she received was nowhere near the amount his wife, Cathy, had gotten when she'd finished her act.

The manager came by, stopping briefly at tables to make sure all was as it should be with the club's service.

"Hi, Doc," Tommy Gardner greeted Dex, tugging at his full beard. "How come you're not home cracking the books?"

"You know what they say about all work and no play, makes for a dull boy."

"Well, have a good evening," the manager said, nodding to Cade. "How about you, sir? Have they taken your order for dinner?"

Cade nodded and the manager moved on to make inquiries of other customers before the music started for the next act.

"Doc?" Cade asked, curious.

"I'm in med school here at Wash. U."

Cade wondered about a doctor having a stripper for a wife. Somehow he expected Cathy was going to become disposable when Dexter got his degree.

The lights dimmed and Ashleigh appeared in the spotlight onstage. She stood statuelike, letting her nude appearance surprise those who, unlike Cade, hadn't seen her act before.

And then she began dressing, doing the cheerleader routine she'd worked out. It was a huge hit as it had been the first time Cade had seen it and it put Dexter in a foul mood.

"I don't see what's so special about her," Dexter snapped when she'd left the stage after the thunderous applause for her routine. "I mean, she's not even blond or anything."

Cade was surprised to find himself rushing to defend Ashleigh. "You have to admit she's got a pretty original routine."

"Yeah? You think that's what it is that works for her?"

Cade nodded.

Dexter seemed pleased.

Puzzled by his reaction at first, Cade figured it out a few minutes later. Dexter had glommed on to the fact that it wasn't Ashleigh who was better than his wife, only her act. Of course, that wasn't what Cade had meant, but he didn't see any harm in letting Dexter console himself with the idea.

Cade's meal came then and Dexter got up to go backstage to talk to his wife. Cade was happy for the chance to eat in peace and observe the club, watching for a glimmer of any impropriety that he could follow up on; an escort service, drugs, anything.

But there was nothing to make him suspect anything more than good old-fashioned lust drawing the customers to Miss Olivia's Finishing School for Young Ladies.

What was the world coming to? he thought sardonically, pushing his plate away.

"Come here often, don't you?" the rumpled-looking blond guy who slid into Dexter's cooled seat asked.

Cade didn't tell him to go screw himself because the blond was one of the chief suspects on Cade's mental list of possible perps of any criminal action that might be going down at the club.

"What?" Cade's voice held authority but no rancor.

"Smoke?" the guy offered, taking out a cigarette.

"I quit."

"Yeah, so have I. Three times. But every time I quit I get blocked." He lit up and took a drag. "I work for the River City *Call*. You might have read my column. I'm Harry Wolfe as in 'Prowling the Night.' It's carried in the everyday entertainment section."

Cade frowned. So much for one of his chief suspects. Harry Wolfe had a legitimate reason for being at the club all the time.

"Rough life," Cade commented on Harry's job.

"If you knew how many boring plays I have to sit through, you wouldn't begrudge me this cushy assignment, pal. I hope it drags on for a bit. I don't know how many more versions of *Show Boat* I can watch at the Muny."

Cade couldn't help the grin that brought to his lips. He had been dragged to a few tired performances by dates himself.

"Well, if Vincent Palmer has his way, this place is going to be closed by the good people of the community faster than you can say 'Take it off.'"

"Yeah, well, Vincent has his nose out of joint because he's been left holding a few Roast Duckling with Blackberry Sauce dinners. But he's going to have to come up with something to compete with Miss Olivia's because they aren't breaking any laws by being open."

"I think it's going to be pretty hard for Vincent to come up with something to compete with naked ladies dancing while you eat," Cade said with a chuckle. "So it looks like you have a pretty good run if he intends to keep picketing the place."

"Let's hope." Harry tossed back the last of the drink he'd brought with him to the table. "I didn't get your name," he said, offering his hand before he moved on.

"I didn't give it," Cade replied. "I don't fancy having my name in your column—no offense."

"Ah, you have some kind of sensitive job . . . or a wife?" Harry asked with a wink.

"Neither. I just like to watch naked ladies in anonymity."

"You and everyone else. Trying to get a name to quote in my column for this story is like trying to find someone to bet against the Dallas Cowboys."

"You might try Dexter Murry," Cade suggested. "His wife is one of the girls working here."

"Onstage?"

"Cathy—"

"Oh, right. The perky blonde. Hey, thanks, pal. I'll do that."

"YOU LOOKED HOT up onstage tonight, baby," Dexter said, pulling his petite blond wife into his arms and kissing her.

"You think so?"

"I know so," he said, kicking the dressing-room door shut with his foot.

"Dexter, we can't fool around in here."

"Okay, okay. But it's all your fault, baby. You are such a pretty little thing. . . ."

Cathy smiled shyly, drinking in the compliment.

"What say we go out dancing when you get off," Dexter suggested.

"Really!" Cathy squealed. Dex hadn't taken her dancing ever.

"Everyone will be jealous of my beautiful wife," Dexter said, kissing her again.

"No, everyone will be jealous of my handsome husband."

Their kissing was interrupted by a knock on the door.

ASHLEIGH ANSWERED the knock on her dressing-room door and saw Cathy standing there.

"Oh, hi, Cathy. Come on in."

Ashleigh returned to the dressing table where she continued taking off her stage makeup.

"I came to ask you a favor," Cathy said, sitting down on the edge of the table after pushing aside a brush.

"Sure. What can I do to help?" Ashleigh tossed a cream-smeared tissue into the trash basket beside her.

"Dexter was talking to Harry Wolfe about me and Dex said he thought I ought to think up a more original routine like you did."

Ashleigh stopped what she was doing. "Dexter? Who's Dexter?"

"Dexter is my husband."

"I didn't know you were married!"

"Yeah, well, Dexter's not around much. I'm dancing here to put him through med school. When he gets his degree I won't have to work at all. I'll be one of those ladies who shop and do lunch. I can't wait. And Dexter's so handsome. He's going to make the prettiest babies."

Ashleigh felt a momentary pang of jealousy at Cathy's happiness.

"Anyway, Dexter took a night off from hitting the books to come watch me dance tonight. He saw your act and thinks I need to make my act more unusual so I don't get lost in the crowd."

"But you got lots of applause," Ashleigh was quick to assure her.

Cathy nodded, pleased that Ashleigh had praised her. "But Dexter's sort of an overachiever. He says I should try harder to be a star performer. He thinks if I come up with something really good, Tommy will pay me more money."

"You mean everyone doesn't get the same pay?" Ashleigh asked in surprise.

"Well, most of us do. Cassie was making more because she used fire in her act. But she was only here for the opening of Miss Olivia's. She came up from one of the other clubs—Dallas, I think."

Ashleigh took her hair down from its ponytail and shook her head. "I think the two of us ought to be able to come up with a new twist for you. Let's put our ideas together after work one night."

"Thanks, Ashleigh." Cathy gave her a quick hug and bounded off to meet Dexter to tell him the good news.

When the door closed behind Cathy, Ashleigh remembered she'd forgotten to ask Cathy about Cade again.

5

AS ASHLEIGH WAITED to go onstage a few nights later, she was a little nervous.

It wasn't because of the lipstick-scrawled message on her dressing-room mirror. She'd decided that was an isolated prank by one of the other strippers who'd given in to a moment of jealousy when Ashleigh's routine had taken the spotlight away from everyone.

If she had to guess who the culprit was, she suspected Trisha. With her long dark hair and exotic looks, she'd been slated to be the feature attraction when Cassie had left. Luckily there hadn't been any other threats. Ashleigh no longer worried about it as she had at first.

Tonight she was nervous because she was debuting her new costume. If it worked, she planned to go to the manager and demand to be paid more than the other girls. That was also increasing the activity of the butterflies in her stomach. She knew her act was drawing record crowds.

She wondered if *he* would be in the audience.

Cade Hawkins turned her butterflies into giant moths when she thought about dancing for him.

He made her dance intimate because she focused on him alone. And because of it he was taking the form of an obsession in her mind. He was never far from her thoughts.

Who was he?

He, too, seemed to focus only on her. Although he was always around, she'd noticed it was her he watched dance.

Had she dismissed him too lightly as the person who'd issued the lipsticked warning? Was he some kind of great-looking nutcase? Was her judgment any good at all?

Was she crazy thinking such thoughts just before going onstage? She needed to feel confident, not confused. So she banished Cade Hawkins from her mind.

Until she took the stage and she saw him sitting there.

Alone at a table.

Watching.

And she began seducing him, drawn to him like she'd never before been drawn to a man.

But Cade wasn't the only one watching Ashleigh. She had the whole room's attention, all eyes on her. Watching her stand motionless in the spotlight, appearing nude before a sexy French song came on and she began her new act, dressing in another male fantasy.

First she put a little lace cap atop her head, its pristine whiteness contrasting with her long dark hair as she curtsied to the audience.

Next came a pair of black fishnet stockings she pulled up slowly to where they stayed snugly at the tops of her thighs, the black lace band sexy against her pale, firm, dancer's thighs, while the fishnet displayed her shapely legs to delicious advantage. All the leg men in the crowd were hooting.

She egged them on with a practiced high kick that might have come from the Folies-Bergères in Paris.

A very abbreviated black silk French maid's dress completed the outfit. When she zipped it up, it accentuated her tiny waist. The neckline scooped low in front and the little skirt just skimmed the tops of her thighs.

Using the French song for atmosphere, she parodied dusting a room with a very provocative feather duster. She was up on her tiptoes dusting the top of an imaginary armoire with her back to the audience, and then facing them, bending ever so low to dust the floorboards. Housework had never been so sexy.

Her use of the feather duster was clever and saucy as she let herself go, and she had the audience enthralled by the end of her number.

Curtsying again, she looked straight at Cade and called out, "*Parlez-vous français?*"

The audience roared back with a great deal of unbridled enthusiasm.

Ashleigh smiled even though Cade Hawkins hadn't responded, had just continued to watch her with a bemused expression on his face.

She put her hand to her ear daintily, cocking her hip to one side as she asked the audience, "*Comment vous appelez-vous?*"

The audience shouted back, "Ashleigh!"

She smiled. Her French-maid costume was the success she'd hoped it would be.

Even if *he* refused to participate. One of these times he wasn't going to be able to remain so aloof. It was a vow she made to herself as she left the stage.

One of these times she was going to wear a little white cap that would heat him up until he melted....

Trisha, who had been watching Ashleigh from backstage, grabbed her and hugged her, then gave her a big kiss on the cheek. "I love your costume," she said.

"Thanks," Ashleigh mumbled, caught by surprise.

Trisha released her to go onstage for her number and Ashleigh went to knock on Cathy's dressing-room door. She wanted to ask Cathy about Cade before she left.

But Cathy didn't answer her knock.

Deciding Cathy's husband might be with her, Ashleigh didn't knock a second time, allowing them their privacy. Heaven knew, a med student didn't have much free time. He'd have to make the best use of it when he had it. She'd ask Cathy about Cade another time.

Back in her own dressing room, she was startled when she looked in the mirror.

The lipstick Trisha had left on her cheek when she'd kissed her was bright red.

"THAT WAS A PRETTY cheeky performance," Cade said as Ashleigh stood at the door of the club waiting for a cab. Her car was in the shop for some routine maintenance.

She didn't answer him.

"You know if you don't quit soon, you're going to really like the money. It's just going to get harder, the longer you put it off," he nagged.

"You mean it might be habit-forming?" she finally said, annoyed by his censure.

"No *might* about it."

Her cab arrived. "You should know, I guess. You seemed to have formed a habit. You practically live here," she retorted over her shoulder as she got into the car.

Cade watched her go, knowing he'd struck a nerve.

Her defensive parting barb had given her away. She was enjoying what she was doing.

And he wasn't prudish enough to deny her that.

Hell, he was enjoying what she was doing.

A little too much. She was distracting him from the reason he was at Miss Olivia's. He wasn't any closer to finding a reason to close down the place than he had been when he'd started the investigation more than a week ago.

In a way he wasn't much better than Harry Wolfe, who was whipping the controversy surrounding the club into much-discussed columns under his "Prowling the Night" byline simply so he could keep ogling the naked ladies. Just because Cade only wanted to ogle *one* naked lady, didn't make him a Boy Scout, even if he did know the salute.

It was time to call in the troops or he was not only going to stay in Vice, he was going to start liking it.

He'd call in markers from J.J., Brown and Allen. Between the four of them, someone was bound to notice something in an evening if anything was go-

ing on. He grinned. Somehow he didn't think it was
going to be difficult to persuade the three of them
to put in a little free time at Miss Olivia's.

He could only hope Monica was out of town.

The manager walked by the pay phone, nodding in recognition as Cade placed a call to J.J.
What, Cade wondered, was Tommy Gardner's
background? Where had he come from? It was time
to run a check on him. You never knew what would
turn up a lead.

CADE WASN'T AT Miss Olivia's the following night.

And Ashleigh's act wasn't quite as good.

No one in the audience noticed, because she went
through all the motions. But she noticed. And it
told her that what she enjoyed had a lot more to do
with Cade Hawkins than she cared to admit.

It was dancing while he watched that turned her
on, not the roomful of people.

And the former was a more dangerous addic-
tion.

After the applause, she left the stage and remembered to try Cathy's dressing room once again.
This time Cathy answered her knock, but she appeared to have been crying.

"What's the matter?"

"It's nothing," Cathy insisted, wiping the back of her hand against her damp cheek. "Dexter and I had a little fight."

"Does he want you to stop working at Miss Olivia's?" Ashleigh guessed.

"Oh, no. No. He needs me to work here. I can't make this much money doing anything else. He just wants me to bring home more. I shouldn't be telling you this," Cathy sniffed.

"Listen, we'll go back to my place tonight and we'll work on a new act for you, okay? Will that make you feel better?"

"Yes, I guess. But I don't want to—"

"I want to," Ashleigh assured Cathy.

"Okay," Cathy agreed.

"I've been wanting to ask you something," Ashleigh said, stretching to get rid of a kink. "What do you know about Cade Hawkins?"

"You mean the hunk?"

"Yeah."

Cathy shrugged. "His name, is about all. Dexter sat with him the other night and said Cade was about as talkative as a fence post."

"You don't know what he does for a living or anything?"

"No. Just that he's a regular." Cathy frowned. "But I don't recall seeing him here tonight."

"I know."

Cathy came up with a smile. "Ah...I get it. You're sweet on him."

"Do I look crazy?" Ashleigh said, asking herself as well as Cathy.

"No, you look smitten."

"Well, I'm not," Ashleigh sniffed.

Cathy didn't bother to hide a knowing grin.

"I'm not." Smitten was too weak a word for what she felt.

THAT EVENING when Ashleigh and Cathy met in the entry to go back to Ashleigh's and plan Cathy's new act, Trisha called out just as they were leaving.

"Tommy said to give you this." Trisha handed Ashleigh an envelope with Ashleigh's name printed on it.

"Thanks." Ashleigh tucked the envelope inside her purse. She didn't want to open it in front of Cathy because she expected it contained the bonus Tommy had promised her for becoming the main attraction at Miss Olivia's.

"Do you want to go by Fatman's and get a barbecue sub sandwich?" Cathy asked. "There's something about taking off my clothes that makes me hungry."

Ashleigh laughed and agreed to a late bite.

Over the barbecued rib-tip sandwiches and mashed potato salad, the two of them worked to change Cathy's act. Ashleigh had noted the booming popularity of magic so she suggested Cathy find a way to incorporate magic into her act.

At first Cathy was intimidated by the idea, but Ashleigh convinced her she could do it and promised to help.

It was after twelve when Ashleigh dropped Cathy back at her car.

As she pulled away, she thought she saw Cade sitting in a car across the street from Miss Olivia's.

But she shook it off as her imagination.

She'd just wanted to see Cade.

He wasn't really there.

CADE SAT IN HIS CAR watching as Ashleigh dropped off Cathy by her car in the parking lot next to Miss Olivia's.

What were the two of them doing out together this late at night after working?

They were still made-up . . . and dressed up.

The two of them hadn't changed into sweats and gone to a movie or anything. The two of them weren't friends of long standing. They'd just met while working at Miss Olivia's, as far as he knew.

He recalled the envelope from the club manager he'd seen Ashleigh tuck into her purse and didn't like the suggestion that came to mind. *Escort service.*

He didn't want Ashleigh involved in the reason he found to close down the club.

He just plain didn't want Ashleigh involved at all.

BACK IN HER APARTMENT Ashleigh put a bluesy Eric Clapton CD in the CD player and cleaned up her apartment. Straightening was what she did when she wasn't in control. And while she was for the first time in control of her life, she wasn't in control of her emotions.

Cade Hawkins's absence from Miss Olivia's had bothered her more than she liked. She couldn't let herself become dependent again. She wouldn't let it happen.

When she'd gathered her laundry, she sorted the whites from the bright colors and tossed a laundry load in the combination washer/dryer in the hall closet.

Next she made the bed with its pale pink sheets and white coverlet. She'd splurged on two-hundred thread-count sheets at the discount store and scrimped by making the dust ruffle and pillow slips herself. She'd felt pleased with herself when she'd found a matching duvet cover to put over an old comforter. Her bed had a cushy feminine look and feel for very little money—which was all she had.

Moving to the living room, she picked up the clutter of catalogs and magazines she'd gleaned ideas for her costumes from and stacked them in baskets she'd bought at a tag sale.

All the while she listened to the music and tried not to think about Cade Hawkins and why he kept nagging her to quit Miss Olivia's. It was both flattering and annoying.

She cleared the cups and saucers, putting them in the dishwasher, and after watering her plants, sat down to make a shopping list.

While she wasn't much of a cook, she was learning.

After a disaster with salt in a batch of cookies, she'd learned to put sugar and salt in different-colored canisters. She now made a mean chocolate-chip cookie, having learned that vegetable shortening was the secret to texture. Piecrust was still way beyond her limited skills, but she had hopes.

If she could learn to strip for a club full of customers, she didn't suppose there was much she couldn't learn.

Thinking of the club made her remember the envelope. Retrieving her purse, she withdrew the envelope to check the amount inside.

When she opened the envelope, she didn't find the expected check, but a note instead.

Printed and brief.

And scary.

It read: "Get out now."

She dropped it as if it would burn her hand, and it fluttered to the carpet.

She bolted up and checked all the locks on the doors and windows of the apartment.

How badly did Cade Hawkins want her to quit?

Was he using scare tactics? Was he the one behind the threats?

He didn't seem the type, but then she was assuming a lot since neither she nor anyone else seemed to know much more about him than his name.

Surely she couldn't be making another bad choice. Not that she'd made a choice, exactly.

Trisha had said Tommy had given her the note for Ashleigh. Had Tommy Gardner written it? That didn't make sense when he'd promised her a bonus and even more important, she was bringing money into the club.

Was Trisha behind it? Jealousy could be a motive. And in Trisha's case it would make sense, even if Trisha was openly friendly to her. That could just be a cover for her true feelings.

For that matter, Cathy or any of the other girls could have left the note in Tommy's office to be passed on to her when he wasn't there.

Ashleigh's ballet experience hadn't been a cake-walk. She'd come across plenty of professional jealousy in dance class—everything from pushy stage mothers to ambitious dancers who would stop at nothing to get the lead role in an important production.

But she hated to think that was what was behind the threatening note. And she couldn't allow her-self to think Cathy was involved.

And there was Vincent Palmer, the leader of the Close Miss Olivia's movement. She had seen the entertainment columnist, Harry Wolfe, having lunch at the coffee shop with Vincent when she'd stopped for a cup of coffee on her way to work. Cade had been there, too, having lunch with a guy who looked like he could have been a linebacker in a former life. They hadn't spoken. She wasn't even sure that he'd noticed her being there at all.

Was Vincent Palmer willing to try threats when his picketing didn't accomplish what he hoped for? He wasn't physically intimidating. But he was scary, in a fanatical sort of way.

Quitting was out of the question. No one was going to scare her away—not when she had found a way to get on with her life.

She decided the best response was to keep the note a secret until she'd investigated what its source might be. If it was just the professional jealousy of one of the other girls, she'd feel like a fool making a big production of it.

Putting the note back in her purse, she got up to take a shower and go to bed. Tomorrow she'd ask the manager about it, and then make her decision on what action to take.

CADE STOPPED BY the police station on his way home.

He wasn't supposed to be working on anything in Homicide. But he had a reputation for not doing what he was supposed to do. So while he was there he was curious enough to check up on a few of the cases he'd been working on, as well as Tommy Gardner.

J.J. had the file for him. Other than a few traffic tickets and an outstanding parking violation, Tommy Gardner was clean. A career as a bouncer had gradually led to managing a club. The club in Clayton was his third and biggest to date.

So it didn't make any sense that Tommy would be running an escort service out of Miss Olivia's.

"Say, when's your old lady coming home, man?" Cade asked as he and J.J. walked to their cars in the parking lot. The air was crisp, the night cool. "Do you live at this place when she's not home?"

"Just about. It keeps me out of trouble, strange as that sounds. But Monica is coming home tomorrow. So don't be looking to see me for a week."

Cade smiled, elbowing his partner. "Have you got something real romantic planned? Champagne, flowers, candy, Luther Vandross—"

"Heck no. All Monica needs is me."

Cade's laugh was deep and rich to his own ears. It was good to be with his friend. "In a pair of monogrammed silk pajamas, right?" Cade teased.

"Don't be talking no trash. She has enough ideas. I draw the line at silk boxers."

Cade rubbed his still-smiling lips. "How could I have a partner with no romance in his soul?"

"My soul is just fine, and you've got enough romance in your pants for the two of us," J.J. said as a car of teens went by with the speakers blasting so loud they shook the air. Both men rolled their eyes. "Speaking of romance, your attorney lady-friend asked about you today when she was in to bail out a perp."

"She's not my friend—"

"Oh, don't go holding a grudge. She got you, man. Got you good. Especially since you're working a Vice detail. She said putting a man who's good with vices like you in Vice was like putting a cat in a canary cage. There's bound to be someone who gets—"

"Could we change the subject, here? I want you and cousins Brown and Allen to make an evening of it at Miss Olivia's."

"I told you Monica will be back in town," J.J. said as they reached his car.

"I know. Bring her. And tell the other two to bring their women, as well. Make an evening of it. Steak dinners, wine and sexy dancers. Then you go home and do what comes naturally. Hell, I'll be doing you a favor."

"Uh-huh. You paying?"

Cade just laughed.

"Okay, what's the other shoe?" J.J. asked, opening the door to his car and leaning against it.

"The other shoe . . . ?"

"Yeah, why you really want us there. What do you suspect is going down at Miss Olivia's that you want us to watch for? Is someone selling drugs? You know you need the narc guys for that—"

"No, I think they may be running an escort service but I don't have any proof. It's just a hunch. I saw two of the girls return to the club a few hours after they left so one of them could pick up her car."

"That's all? Oh, for Pete's sake, Cade. You're grasping at straws to get back into Homicide. Just let the captain cool down. You'll be back."

"Ashleigh may be involved."

"Who's Ashleigh?" J.J. frowned, then remembered and grinned. "Oh, *Ashleigh*."

"She's just a nice girl," Cade defended. At least he really hoped she was. Surely he had some judgment when it came to women that wasn't led by his, well . . . libido.

"A nice girl who takes off her clothes in public," J.J. said, shaking his head.

"You'll come to the club . . . ?"

"I'll talk to Monica, that's all I'll promise. I'm not getting into any arguments with her for you and winding up sleeping on the couch. I love you, pal, but . . ."

"Yeah. I know. Love and sex are two different things, right?"

"No, not when you find the right woman," J.J. said, voicing his first serious thought in their conversation. "I keep telling you that."

"Yeah, yeah. All you married guys just want to spoil the fun for us single guys. You want us to have to—"

"Know what Luther is singing about," J.J. supplied. "Trust me, Cade, when it's love, it's a whole other thing. It's cosmic or something, I don't know."

"And I think your Monica's been out of town on that buying trip too long, that's what I think."

"And maybe Ashleigh is the one who'll make you see what you've been missing. Though word is you ain't been missing much, pal."

"Just because I'm on a diet, J.J., doesn't mean I can't look at the menu."

"Yeah, well, just make sure you don't sample it."

J.J. closed his car door and waved as he drove away.

A half hour later Cade pulled into his own driveway. Shadow wasn't at the front door to meet him despite the late hour.

He knew exactly where Shadow would be. He was hiding behind the bed in the bedroom. And he wouldn't come out until he was sure it was Cade who'd entered the house.

"It's me, boy. Daddy's home," Cade called out, loud enough for his voice to carry to the bedroom.

Sure enough, there was the sound of Shadow's nails clicking against the hardwood floor as he bounded down the hallway to greet him, barking joyfully, his tail wagging a breeze around him as Cade petted the silly coward.

"You're some watchdog, you know that, boy. Burglars could break in here and you'd show them where the family jewels were hidden."

Shadow was on his back, whining and doing just that, soaking up the attention after being alone in the house for so long. Cade felt so damn guilty he left the TV on all day. Even checked the listings to see what channel "Lassie" was on. No one knew that. J.J. and the guys would have a field day with that little nugget of information.

The truth was, Cade was just as happy to see Shadow as the dog was to see him.

Maybe there was something to that love business J.J. kept talking about.

"What do you think, boy? Do we need a wife?"

Cade didn't know about a wife, but he did need more in his life than he had.

More than a job he loved.

More than J.J. and Monica.

More than Shadow.

He needed a woman he could talk to before, during and after. A woman who would love a cop.

A foolish woman.

6

ASHLEIGH DANCED to a Mendelssohn duet, arching forward and back in one motion, taking two counts to get her head down to her legs with her knees straight. Though her dreams of being a ballerina had been dashed, she still danced a half hour or so a day. The side benefits were a flat tummy, taut buttocks, firm breasts and being able to eat dessert every day.

If only she could control her life the way she could exercise control over her lithe dancer's body. Unfortunately, the stretches, bends, jumps and turns of the physically draining workout weren't enough to take her mind off the threatening note in her purse. The discipline of ballet wasn't working; she couldn't tune out her situation.

In a final effort to empty her mind of her immediate worries, she focused instead on completing her dance routine for her act at the club.

Soon finished with her practice, Ashleigh showered and then headed for a coffee and dessert at the coffee shop before she was due at Miss Olivia's.

The coffee shop was bustling with a late-afternoon crowd—those from the police station and courthouse located nearby who were grabbing a late lunch or early dinner because of their erratic schedules.

Crime didn't keep regular hours.

Ashleigh lucked into a table after a five-minute wait. Having ordered a cup of Colombian gourmet blend and a slice of fresh fruit cobbler, she began doodling on her napkins . . . sketching an idea for another outfit. She knew she had to keep her act interesting by varying the costumes, so she had to build up a collection.

Her reason for stopping at the coffee shop was twofold: a sweet tooth and another sort of hankering. Cade Hawkins had followed her here once, and maybe . . .

What if calling him a regular at Miss Olivia's had offended him and he never came back? What if she never saw him again? She'd gotten used to him being there in the crowd when she danced.

Had liked him being there in the crowd.

With him watching she felt sexy when she danced. He'd awakened her in a new and exciting way without ever laying a hand on her.

She drew the model—small head, broad shoulders, impossibly long legs—as she'd been taught in fashion-design classes, then began and discarded several rough sketches of costumes on the tidy pile of napkins she'd pulled from the napkin holder. Each outfit she drew evolved into something a bit different.

Her head bent lower as she became engrossed, excited about the idea taking hold. Her felt-tip pen moved rapidly so she could transfer her idea to the hastily devised paper before she lost it. She knew from experience you had to grab inspiration when it grabbed you. If you waited, it disappeared and never came back—at least not in the exact same detail.

Ideas were like men; you had to pay close attention or they tended to drift away.

She continued sketching, the felt marker in her hand laying down sharp black slashes in rapid succession.

And then she stopped, her pen stilled.

Someone was watching her.

She could feel it. The fine hairs on the back of her neck were rising to alert her. Was it the person who'd written her the two warning messages?

Slowly, she lifted her head and began a careful perusal of the coffee shop. The customers were strangers, although some looked vaguely familiar, no doubt because she'd seen them in stores, or even at the club.

Her eyes stopped when they came to a table at the back of the room. Two men sat there, their heads close together, deep in conversation. The one with the goatee was gesturing excitedly.

She recognized him as one of the restaurant owners opposed to Miss Olivia's. The blond man with him was the reporter, Harry Wolfe. Somehow Ashleigh knew Harry wasn't going to have much difficulty getting a controversial statement from the owner of Vincent's.

"Come here often, do you?"

Ashleigh nearly jumped out of her chair at the sound of Cade's voice just behind her. She turned, trying not to show how happy she was to see him.

"You still following me?" she asked.

"If you like," he said, turning her retort around and making her sound like she'd been fishing for a compliment. She felt herself blush.

He took a chair, not asking politely this time as he had the first. And then he was audacious enough to slide the chair around the table so that he was sitting next to her at the two-person table, instead of across from her. It was a bold move, a high school cafeteria move. And he waited for her to call him on it.

She wouldn't give him the satisfaction of noticing.

"What do you want?" she asked, stacking the napkins she'd been sketching on.

"That looks good," he commented on the cup of steaming coffee and slice of cobbler the waitress set in front of Ashleigh. "I'll have the same." The waitress nodded and left.

"I don't recall inviting you to join me...."

He just sat there, grinning—no...more half smirk, half grin and all innuendo, mixed with a dollop of invitation. To what she didn't have to guess. Cade Hawkins was made for women. He was a sight for sore eyes, as the saying went, and an even better one for fresh eyes.

And her eyes were very fresh.

The half grin, half smirk became a full-fledged smirk, telegraphing he wasn't unaware of her appraisal and his effect on her. But it also signaled his interest in her.

"You know, I'm really hungry. I fed my dog this morning, but I forgot to eat." He eyed her warm cobbler with whipped cream.

She slipped a bite of her cobbler into her mouth and chewed slowly, making it look like the best thing she'd ever eaten.

"That's not very hospitable, you know," he said, looking pitiful.

"Funny, I don't *recall* inviting you to—"

"Sugar pie, you've been inviting all kinds of things in my mind when I watch you dance."

Swallowing the cobbler was going to be nearly impossible.

"Well, I'm not responsible for what you think," she said finally, tugging at the hem of her dark green sweatshirt.

"Would you like to know what I—"

"*No!*"

And here she thought she should have gone with the nurse costume when he'd failed to show up. Thought he'd lost interest . . . that she'd failed to hold his attention.

"Give me a little bite, please. . . ."

She offered her fork—anything to change the subject.

"No, feed me. It'll taste better. You know, the personal touch and all." He was all risqué humor and dare. His tongue played with the inside of his cheek, provoking her.

She wanted to kick him under the table and tell him to behave.

Instead she gave in and fed him a piece of her cobbler. He put his hand on hers as he slipped the pie from her fork with his mouth. It took a moment longer than necessary for him to release her hand.

A speck of whipped cream sat on the corner of his lip.

She felt her tongue search out the very place on her own mouth. Saw him notice.

And she blushed yet again.

He flicked the speck of whipped cream from his lip with his forefinger and offered it to her.

She shook her head.

His eyes accused, "Chicken." He put his finger in his mouth and sucked.

The sexual tension between them was so thick it would have taken a chain saw to sever it.

"I don't—" she began.

"Shut up, and kiss me."

She gasped, caught completely by surprise.

He grinned, and winked. "I heard that in a song on the radio."

And then he slipped his hand beneath her long hair to cup the back of her neck, bringing her mouth to his.

She would have protested, not used to public displays of affection, but he'd taken her breath away, kissing her senseless. Kissing her so sexily and sweetly it curled her toes and made her ears tingle.

"Um . . ." he murmured, his lips releasing hers. "I was afraid of that."

"What?"

"That I'd want to do it some more."

Ashleigh fought to break free of the spell he seemed to have put her under. She was helped by the waitress, who showed up with Cade's order.

"Anything else?" the waitress asked innocently.

"Yeah, but I think I'll restrain myself—for now." Cade winked at Ashleigh.

The waitress laid down the tab and moved on to another table.

"What are you drawing?" Cade nodded at the stack of napkins she'd put by her purse.

"I plan to be a fashion designer."

"And you think Miss Olivia's is a career path to fashion design?" he asked, sipping his coffee.

"In a way. I've got some debts to pay off. My ex-husband ran amok with our credit cards."

"Ex-husband. You've been married? Kinda young for that, aren't you?"

He'd said it like he thought anyone under eighty was.

"As it turned out, yes. I won't make the same mistake again. I like being my own boss."

Cade forked a piece of cobbler into his mouth. "How long you planning to work at Miss Olivia's?" he asked. "Do you have any experience in fashion design?"

"I have a year of school and talent. Once I've paid off the debt, I guess I'll find out how much."

J.J. would love this, Cade thought. He'd hooked up with a woman like his Monica who was interested in fashion. Maybe he'd better cut back on the ribbing he dished out to his partner.

"You didn't say how long—"

"You mean Miss Olivia's?" Ashleigh shrugged. "A while." She hadn't allowed herself to think about it.

"I still think you'll get used to the money and then it will be hard to give it up."

"Apparently you aren't listening. There is no money to get used to. I'm paying off my ex-husband's debt, and then I'm outta there. It's not exactly a job you retire from, you know."

Cade laughed. "You've got me there."

"How about you? Any ex-wives? A current one?"

"I wouldn't have kissed you like that if there was a current one," he assured her. "I've never been married. It's just me and my dog."

"That's a hopeful sign," she said, smiling at him.

"What is?"

"That you have a dog. It's a sign of sociability."

"I have friends," he said, looking affronted.

"Haven't seen you with any."

"I could say the same about you."

"I've made friends with Cathy," she countered. "Or I guess you could say she's made friends with me. It's hard not to be friends with Cathy."

"You two spend a lot of time together, then?" Cade asked, switching into cop mode, and not liking himself for it.

"A little. She has time on her hands since her husband is in med school."

"Yeah, I met him. He's a real prince." Sarcasm dripped from Cade's voice.

"You don't like him?"

"I don't like him."

"Why?"

"Because he's living off a woman he plans to ditch as soon as he becomes a doctor."

"He told you that?"

"He didn't have to."

Ashleigh didn't argue with him. She had the same gut feeling about Dexter Murry.

Cade pushed his dessert plate away and tilted Ashleigh's chin so she looked at him. Then, taking a deep breath, he asked, "Tell me something, Ashleigh. If I wanted to date you, do I ask you—or Tommy Gardner?"

She just stared at him, puzzled.

And then it dawned on her exactly what Cade was asking her.

He thought she was going to slap his face.

She didn't. She teared up. Fought them back. Controlled them long enough to pick up the tab.

She reached for her purse but he stilled her hand.
"No, I'll get it. Listen, Ashleigh, I had to ask."

"Well, you asked."

Getting up, she walked out of the coffee shop
without looking back.

He wished she'd slapped him.

ASHLEIGH CLOSED the door to her dressing room,
wishing she could close out the world.

Tommy, of course, hadn't known where the envelope Trisha had given her had come from.
Someone, he didn't recall who, had given it to him
and he'd passed it on to her because her name was
printed on it.

The tears that had threatened at the coffee shop
now broke through to a sob. Damn. She wiped
them away, angry at her show of weakness.

Sitting before the dressing table, she took the
note from her purse. After glancing at the warning
a final time, she crumpled the paper and tossed it
in the trash can beside her.

Cade had insulted her.

Someone had threatened her.

But she wasn't leaving. Not until she was ready.
Not until she'd paid off all of the debt and she was
free to pursue her own life.

HE WAS BACK.

Where had he gotten the nerve?

He was sitting at a table with a handsome couple, as if nothing had happened. It probably was nothing to him.

She bit her lip to keep the tears that wanted to surface at bay. So he thought she was that kind of woman, did he? Well, she'd give him that sort of woman. She was going to steam the mauve and blue Art Deco wallpaper right off the walls with her number.

She sold the French-maid theme to everyone in the club. The men all wanted her, and the women all wanted to be her. The applause was sustained a long, gratifying time.

Cade's face looked like a thundercloud.

The pretty woman in the designer suit beside him was whispering something in his ear. She wondered if she was Cade's date. If she was, Cade was dating a very attractive woman with a great flair for fashion.

In spite of everything, Ashleigh felt a pang of jealousy.

She suddenly couldn't wait to get offstage and back to her dressing room.

"WHAT DO YOU MEAN you don't have a new act yet?" Dexter demanded. "I thought you said you were going to work on one with Ashleigh."

"It takes time, Dex," Cathy explained. "We came up with an idea, but—"

Dexter flung himself down on the club chair by the tiny window in Cathy's dressing room, his displeasure poisoning the air.

"I'm trying, baby," Cathy said, coming over to comfort him, to cheer him on as she always did when he got down about not having enough money.

He shoved her away.

"It's not good enough. Maybe I need to find me a woman who is smart enough to make some real money," he threatened, knowing how it scared Cathy. "Yeah, maybe that's what I need to do. You don't care enough about me to—"

"Dexter, don't talk like that. I love you. You know I'd do anything for you."

"Well, you talk a good story. That's what you do," he said, getting up in disgust.

He opened her closet and flipped through her costumes. "I don't see anything new in here. You aren't even trying, are you?" He tossed the costumes one by one on the floor, dismissing them.

"Dexter!" Cathy cried, picking them up.

"I thought you said you came up with an idea," he challenged, turning on her.

"We did. It's a great idea. Really, it is. Ashleigh suggested that I learn magic."

"What?"

"Magic, Dexter. I know it will take a while, but I think it's a good investment for my act. Magic is big in Las Vegas."

"Yeah, well, this isn't Vegas and you aren't Sigfried or Roy. You're just stupid. Don't you get it? Ashleigh doesn't want the competition. The only magic is that your brain disappeared."

Cathy snapped.

"There's nothing wrong with my brain. I'm just as smart as you are."

"Sure, you are. That's why I'm a doctor and you're a stripper," he sneered.

"You aren't a doctor yet."

"But I will be. And when I am, you're—"

"I'm what, Dexter?"

"Nothing. Just forget it," he retorted, slamming the door of her dressing room on his way out.

He was having another of his temper tantrums. It would blow over. They always did.

And he was always sorry.

But not as sorry as he was going to be this time, Cathy vowed, as she got ready for her dance.

He'd almost voiced her greatest fear. Voiced what she knew was going to happen, deep down in her gut. Dexter was using her. He planned to dump her.

She wasn't going to allow it.

Everyone tended to underestimate her because she was blond and tiny.

A KNOCK SOUNDED on Ashleigh's dressing-room door. It was not going to be her night to be left alone to pout.

She went to the door.

"Trisha . . ." she said, surprised.

"Have you seen this?" Trisha asked, coming into the dressing room with the River City *Call*. She had the everyday section in her hand and it was folded to Harry Wolfe's column. "He's not going to quit until he turns public sentiment against the club. One way or another, Vincent Palmer is going to put Miss Olivia's out of business. I spent a lot of money moving here from Iowa and now it looks like the job is going to go up in smoke."

Ashleigh scanned the column. "I wouldn't pay too much attention to what you read in the newspaper. That's just Harry trying to keep the story going so he can hang out and watch the girls."

"I don't know," Trisha said, taking back the paper. "I overheard Tommy talking to his boss on the phone and he said he thought they might need to do something to bolster the club's image."

Ashleigh laughed. "Like what?"

"Maybe serve caviar dip on the tables or something—that would get Vincent's goatee to curl, wouldn't it? Well, gotta go. I'm on next. It sounded like you did great. Did you design another new costume?"

Ashleigh shook her head no. "I guess I'm getting over being shy is all." Shy? She'd been a real vixen onstage tonight because of her jealous pique. She didn't know where the vixen had come from, but she'd been very effective.

She waved Trisha off, and began freshening her makeup.

Looking in the mirror, she sighed. Probably to hunky private eyes like Cade Hawkins, vixens were an everyday occurrence. The woman at his table was certainly hot looking.

And then she brightened, thinking that maybe the woman had been a client and not a date.

Yeah, and lottery winners weren't going to quit their day jobs.

Another knock sounded at her dressing-room door.

She almost didn't answer it.

But deciding it might be the club manager maybe having heard what was in the envelope she'd gotten, she went to the door.

It was Cade.

"Hi," he said, looking as tempting as chocolate in the dark, slouchy suit he wore so casually on his tall, lean frame.

She would have slammed the door in his face—almost did—before she noticed he wasn't alone.

"Could we come in for a minute?" Cade asked, stepping back so she could see the two people with him. "I've got someone here who wants to meet you."

It was the man and woman who'd been at Cade's table. She wanted to say no. But she was too curious about the woman.

Opening the door wider, she gestured them inside her dressing room.

Cade made the introductions: "Ashleigh, I'd like you to meet my friends—J.J. and his wife, Monica."

Some of the tension eased out of Ashleigh's body at the word "wife" and she smiled, shaking their hands.

"Ashleigh was studying to be a ballerina," Cade said, while Ashleigh tried to recall if she'd told him that. Maybe she'd told someone else who'd told him. But why would he be asking someone questions about her? And then she remembered she was angry with him—and why.

"I grew too tall," Ashleigh said. "But I am a dancer, I guess you could say."

J.J.'s big grin validated her assumption.

"Monica liked your costume," Cade said.

"Yes, I wanted to ask where you'd bought it," J.J.'s wife added. "It's quite something. *Très chic*, if you don't mind my saying so."

"I designed and made it myself," Ashleigh answered.

Monica nodded, tucking one side of her dark bob behind her ear to reveal a smart gold shell earring. "Did you design and make the nude bodysuit you start your number with, as well?"

Ashleigh nodded, happy with the praise from such a beautiful, poised woman.

"Ashleigh wants to go into fashion design," Cade supplied. "I think she's got real talent and I thought if you thought so, too, she'd love hearing it. Monica is a fashion buyer for a chain of boutiques across the country."

"Really?" Ashleigh forgot all about Cade for the moment, focusing on Monica.

"It's true," Monica replied, as J.J. and Cade examined the cache of makeup on the dressing table like mischievous small boys. "I just got back from a buying trip. And to tell you the truth, I didn't see anything as original as what you're doing. I know the French maid outfit is a costume, but fashion is very costumey now. And the nude bodysuit is fabulous."

"Well, I appreciate you coming back to encourage me," Ashleigh said, wishing she were wearing something trendier than a bathrobe.

Monica looked so sexy and fashionable in her suspender pantsuit. The jacket had a boxy, unstructured shape and the cuffed miniplaid trousers had black suspenders that stood out against the white bodysuit she wore underneath.

Ashleigh liked Monica and her sense of style, and felt very complimented and validated.

"Keep at your designing," Monica encouraged. "I think you will do very well."

"Thank you. I plan to."

Ashleigh was about to ask how they had become friends when Cathy rushed into the dressing room, sobbing.

"Cathy, what's wrong!" Ashleigh had never seen the usually upbeat Cathy anywhere near tears before.

"It's . . . it's Dex. . . . He . . . he . . . pushed me against the wall and then he hit me with his fist."

There was no look of surprise on Cade's face, as he muttered something about bullies and shot a glance at his friend J.J.

"Why would someone hit a little thing like you?" Ashleigh asked. "Here, let me see." She coaxed Cathy's hand away from her face.

Monica gasped at the ugly purple bruise on her cheek. "Oh, my word. J.J., go arrest the jerk."

"No," Cathy objected. "He's not here. He slammed out after he hit me."

"Honey, you need a good attorney," Monica said, outraged at a man doing such a thing. Her J.J. was a mountain of a man, but gentle as a golden retriever.

"You need a divorce," Ashleigh said, running some cold water from the ice bucket on her dressing table over a cloth to put on Cathy's cheek.

"I don't know any attorneys," Cathy said, her usually tough voice sounding very soft and lost.

"Cade does," J.J. offered.

"Oh, no, she's not number one on my hit parade," Cade objected.

"Come on, Cade. Melodie Fortune specializes in abuse cases. She'll handle it in a minute or refer her to someone good. Give Cathy her number."

They all stared at him, waiting.

"Aw, hell," he said, writing a number down on a piece of paper. He was never going to be able to forget Melodie Fortune putting one over on him, but there was no reason to take it out on Cathy.

As Miss Olivia's closed down for the night a lone figure remained outside. A sliver of white moon in the inky sky silhouetted the man searching the Dumpster in the alley behind the nightclub. He was neatly dressed and very methodical. Since he didn't know what he was looking for, he examined every item he removed from the sacks of trash in the bin very closely.

It was dirty, nasty work—just like what went on inside Miss Olivia's, he thought with a wild cackle.

But it had paid big dividends in the past, so he kept at the unsavory task.

Only two full plastic sacks of trash remained.

Two last chances.

Then there was just one.

But that was all he needed to strike pay dirt. He found what he'd been searching for in the last plastic sack. A police siren sounded in the night, giving chase and muffling the lone figure's cry, "Eureka."

As far as he was concerned he'd struck gold.

Just like Miss Olivia's had.

THE RINGING PHONE startled Cade out of a deep sleep. He shoved Shadow's paws off his legs so he could get out of bed without waking the dog.

Locating the phone under the bed, Cade picked it up and slumped down on the floor.

"Cade, is that you?"

"What do you want?" he growled.

"I must have woken you, sorry. I was just calling to offer to buy you coffee at the coffee shop by the courthouse in the morning as a thank-you for refer-ring a new client to me."

"What?"

"Cathy Murry called me—"

"At this time of night?"

"She called to leave a message and I just happened to be in my office working, so I picked up. I'm seeing her tomorrow."

"Oh."

"So you'll meet me for coffee in the morning, then?"

"Melodie, it's one in the morning," Cade said and hung up.

It wasn't enough that Melodie Fortune won all her cases, she had to rub it in.

7

"WHY ARE WE HERE?"

"I'm assuming you aren't speaking existentially," Pamela, the dancer with the shag haircut, answered Trisha.

While Cathy wore makeup to cover the bruise on her cheek, the rest of the women were barefaced and dressed casually for the 10:00 a.m. meeting with the club manager.

"Do you think Tommy's called us in to tell us they've decided to close down the club because of all the pickets we keep having to walk past?" Ashleigh wondered aloud. She looked around at the other girls, knowing how the loss of income would affect them, as well. "Maybe the chain doesn't want all the negative publicity that's being generated by the controversy over a strip club operating in a fashionable business district. Maybe this town is too conservative to accept what works in other places," Ashleigh suggested.

"They aren't going to close it down," Cathy disagreed. "The place is packed every night. Businesses do not close down a moneymaker like this club is. I promise you it has to be some other reason Tommy's assembled us. Maybe they're going to start opening for lunch as well as dinner. That would be great. We could double our income."

"Not me," Peggy, the newest girl, said. "I've got classes all day at the college. As soon as I get my degree, I'm outta here. Unless I meet a rich doctor first. Then I'm outta here even sooner."

"Here comes Tommy now, so I guess we'll know soon enough," Cathy said, touching the bruise on her cheek tenderly.

"Does it still hurt?" Ashleigh whispered.

"Not as much as it's going to hurt Dex's wallet when my attorney gets through with him. Melodie Fortune is going to get me a fortune. I don't know where he gets off, thinking he can just—"

"Good morning, ladies," Tommy said, joining them. "Won't you please come into my office. I think we have something to discuss that concerns all of you."

"Oh, are we late?" Bitsy and Mitsy, the twin redheads who only danced on weekends because they commuted from out of town, rushed in just as Tommy was about to close the door.

"You're excused for being tardy since you have an hour's drive to get here," Tommy said, tugging at his mustache. Like most men with facial hair, he had a fondness for touching it. Ashleigh guessed in

Tommy's case he was just checking to make sure it was still there and hadn't deserted him like the hair on his head.

When they were all inside, Tommy took his briefcase and set it on his black lacquer desk, snapping open the slim leather designer case. He withdrew the newspaper that was folded up inside.

"Has anyone read the morning paper yet?" he asked, waving it in front of them.

He was greeted with a chorus of no's.

"Well, I did. I read the front page, and the sports section and then I opened it to the entertainment section to have a look at 'Prowling the Night' to see if Harry Wolfe had finally given it a rest. Guess what?"

"He interviewed some more restaurant and shop owners?" Peggy offered, wanting to get the meeting over with as she had studying to do and a class she was skipping to be there.

"No.

"Anybody else want to tell me what they think Harry has to say in his column?"

"Why doesn't he just tell us?" Cathy whispered to Ashleigh.

"I don't know, but I don't like the sound of this," Ashleigh whispered back.

"No one, huh?"

The women were silent, puzzled about what he was getting at.

"No one had a secret little interview with Harry?" Tommy coaxed, pushing the gilt-and-chrome-framed picture of his brother's family to one side of his desk so he could spread the newspaper out flat for everyone to see the column he was referring to.

If anyone had, they weren't talking.

Tommy looked around the room at each of them.

"Has anyone got anything they want to tell us? Something they should have told me instead of Harry Wolfe, for Pete's sake," he said, slamming his palm on the newspaper.

The women in the room looked at each other in confusion and then back at Tommy.

"Uh, Tommy, we don't know what you're talking about," Cathy said.

"Where'd you get that bruise?" he asked, seeing it for the first time through her makeup.

"I walked into a door," Cathy explained. "What's in Harry's column that's got you all fired up?"

"The fact that one of you—or maybe more, I don't know—has been receiving threatening notes."

"What?" Peggy demanded.

The women all started talking at once except Ashleigh, who stood silent and pale.

"Well?" Tommy prompted, waiting.

It was quiet in the room then, as all the women shook their heads in a negative fashion.

All except Ashleigh.

Cathy picked up on it at once.

"Ashleigh—did you?"

Everyone's attention swung to Ashleigh.

"I didn't talk to Harry."

"Okay, but then why the hell didn't you talk to me? I want to know everything that goes on in this club," Tommy said, dropping down in the black leather chair behind his desk.

It was quiet again as Ashleigh's news sank in.

"What did the note say?" Tommy asked. "Harry says it was a threat. I want to see the note," Tommy declared. It wasn't a request.

"I don't have it anymore. I threw it away," Ashleigh answered.

"What did the note say? Can you at least tell me that?"

"It said, 'Get out now.'"

"That's it?"

Ashleigh nodded.

"Okay, Ashleigh, I want to talk to you. The rest of you ladies can go now. *But*, if any of you get any threats of any kind, I want to know about it. Do you understand?" They all murmured their assent as they filed out of the manager's office.

"Take a seat," Tommy said, closing the door to his office.

"I'd rather stand," Ashleigh replied, suddenly nervous. She'd tried to block the threats from her mind and had partly succeeded, but now Tommy was forcing her to admit that someone wanted her gone.

"Suit yourself." Tommy returned to the chair behind his desk and sat down. "Tell me about it."

"There's not much to tell. First there was—"

"First? You mean there was more than *one* note?" Tommy leaned forward in his chair.

"There was another on the mirror in my dressing room. Someone wrote on it in red lipstick."

"What did it say?"

"'Get out.'"

"Wordy bastard," Tommy muttered.

"Maybe it's just a prank," Ashleigh offered, trying to make light of it. She didn't want to bring up the possibility of it being one of the other dancers.

She didn't have to. Tommy did.

"Do you have an idea that one of the dancers would do something like this? Have you had any set-tos with any of them?"

"No. Of course not," she said. Tommy had spent time on the street. She didn't know anything about "set-tos."

"The note was in the envelope I gave to Trisha for you, wasn't it?"

Ashleigh nodded.

"I'm going to look into this. I will find out who's at the bottom of this one way or another. And I want you to tell me if any more threats of any kind show up. Do you understand me? It may only be professional jealousy since no specific threats were made. But you can't be sure. And until I am, I think it's wise to be cautious."

"Can I go now?" Ashleigh asked, suddenly not feeling so good.

Tommy nodded, looking down at the newspaper once again, frowning as he read Harry's column.

As she left the club, Ashleigh felt mixed emotions; she was relieved that the others knew about the threatening notes. But that same fact also made the situation seem more real.

Someone was watching her. Scaring her.

Who? And why?

CADE HAWKINS was waiting for her outside her apartment building.

He had on a wheat-colored Nantucket sweater and faded jeans that looked...good. He stood leaning against his car, his cowboy boots crossed at the ankle.

When she got out of her car, she headed for her apartment, pretending not to notice him.

He caught up with her, shoving the morning newspaper under her nose. "When were you planning to tell me?"

She brushed past him. "I don't know what you're talking about."

He grabbed her arm, stopping her. "Yes, you do."

She looked from him to the newspaper and then back up at him. She was in no mood for one of his I-told-you-so lectures.

"You should have told me," he reiterated.

"Why? What are you, a cop?" she demanded, pulling her arm free.

"*Yes.*"

Ashleigh felt her jaw drop. "But I thought you were a private eye. You said you were investigating the club when we first met."

"That's because I let you think I was a private eye. I didn't tell you I was a cop because I'm working undercover."

"On what?"

"I can't tell you."

"How convenient. But it has something to do with Miss Olivia's, right?"

Cade nodded.

"Now, about you—" he said, thrusting his hand through his dark hair. "Is there something you want to tell me?"

"Like what?" she asked, not certain how she felt about the news that Cade was a cop. Not only was he an older man, he was an authority figure. She'd been trying to get both out of her life.

"Like whether you have any ideas about who might have been behind the threats you've been receiving. Like whether or not the threats are something new in your life since you began working at the club." Cade stood with his hands on his hips, frustration obvious in his stance.

"How did you know *I* was the one who received the threats?"

Cade shrugged. "I didn't. Until now. But since you're the main attraction . . ."

"Is this official business? Was that insulting question you asked me at the coffee shop official business? Tell me, Cade, why should I tell you anything?"

"Because I want to help. I can help you. And because I don't want to see you get hurt."

"I don't think the threats are anything. . . ."

"Threats have to be taken seriously. I know you think it's one of the girls acting out of momentary jealousy. And it may well be. But there are lots of scary people in the world—other possibilities you might not have considered."

"I don't know..." she said, weakening. Maybe he was only trying to scare her. If he was, it was working.

"Think about it," Cade pleaded. "There are lots of possibilities. You cross a picket line to get into Miss Olivia's. The restaurant owners and shopkeepers are upset. Vincent Palmer is at the top of my list of suspects. He's the one keeping everything whipped up.

"And what do you know about Tommy Gardner, the club manager? He might have leaked the threats to Harry Wolfe, knowing he would publish the information and garner more publicity for the club.

"Harry Wolfe," Cade continued. "He's another possibility. The threats keep the people reading his column. Keep him at Miss Olivia's—which he seems to like.

"And it might not be one of the other dancers behind this but one of their boyfriends or husbands. Dexter Murry, for example," he said, naming Cathy's husband. "A man who'd hit a tiny thing like her, would do most anything. He could be upset because you're the main attraction and not Cathy. That could be what he took out on her."

"You *are* a cop," Ashleigh said, impressed by his impromptu assessment of the situation.

"So take my advice and let me protect you. I want you to—"

"No."

"What's wrong with you? Haven't you been listening to a word I've been saying? You could be in a great deal of danger. I haven't even brought up the fact that this could be a nutcase—"

"No one is going to tell me what I can or can't do," Ashleigh interrupted stubbornly, her chin lifted in defiance. "I have spent my entire life doing what others thought best for me. Now I'm deciding what I want to do. And you or some nutcase are not going to change my plans." That said, she stalked off to her apartment.

Cade didn't try to stop her.

He knew a temper tantrum when he saw one.

He knew a frightened woman when he saw one.

He knew a determined woman when he saw one.

Ashleigh was angry, scared and pissed.

Even he knew better than to tangle with her until she'd cooled down and thought things through. When she did, he was certain she'd come to the same conclusion he had.

She needed him.

THE DRY DOCK BAR was trashed from the retirement party.

The orange and red balloons were half flat and listlessly floating from the yellow and purple crepe-paper streamers stuck over the mirror behind the bar in haphazard fashion.

Cade, J.J. and Captain Gavin were at a table near the front door, one of the few tables still occupied. The bar had been packed to capacity earlier in honor of one of Homicide's best cops. Max Parker was taking early retirement at forty-five after marrying a woman half his age and having his first child.

There had been a lot of ribbing about his being a househusband. He'd told them they were all jealous because he had invested wisely and could retire.

All that was left of the evening of destressing for a lot of street-weary cops was the faint echo of laughter coming from Cade's table as the three considered the color scheme of the decorations.

"Promise me one thing, guys," the captain said, eyeing the red, orange, yellow and purple mix of balloons and streamers. "Promise me you won't send Allen and Brown to decorate when I retire."

"Hell, you'll never retire. Who you going to yell at?"

"He's got you there, Captain," J.J. said laughing.

"I wouldn't laugh if I were you," the older man replied, running his hand over his bald head. "I'm not the one wearing—how would you describe that tie, anyway?"

"It's navy blue with pink polka dots, okay?" J.J. said, defending his wife's taste, if reluctantly.

"Don't let him kid you, Captain," Cade said. "He had a pink lemonade and I shook it up before he opened it, when he wasn't looking. It exploded all over his navy tie."

"I'm glad you guys know your fashion," J.J. said dryly, as the two men convulsed over their own joke.

"Hey, Dave and Rick, you want to help me throw these two bums out?" J.J. called to two of the owners working the bar.

"How about we throw all three of you out?" Rick suggested. "We need to get home before dawn. There must be a doughnut shop still open where you can join the rest of your pals...."

"Let's throw *them* out," J.J. said, standing and pretending offense at the cop joke.

"*You* throw them out. I'm going home to my pipe and slippers," the captain said, pushing back his chair.

"And I'm going home to my dog," Cade added, rising.

"You two go on ahead. I'm going to settle up the bill with Dave and Rick, and hear about Dave's date with that beauteous brunette," J.J. said.

"What about Monica? I'm surprised you didn't leave early. How come you're still here with her home?" Cade asked.

"We had a little spat."

"Uh-oh—"

"It's nothing. All I said was maybe she ought to think about taking a dance class to relax from the stress of her job."

Cade slapped J.J.'s arm. "Not a wise move, pal, after inviting her to a night at Miss Olivia's."

"Where do you think I got the idea?"

"I'd buy roses if I were you. They always add a little something to the 'I'm sorry, please forgive me for being such an animal . . . and now can we have sex?' apology."

"Good idea," J.J. said, brightening as he and the captain left, with Dave waving them off.

When they were outside The Dry Dock the captain turned to Cade. "Do you think you've learned your lesson?"

"What?" Cade asked, caught off guard.

"I'm thinking of pulling you off the Vice detail since you haven't been able to find anything. I'm a man short in the department, with Parker retiring. The chief's going to have to find a zoning law or something to close down the club."

"Don't pull me off Vice now, Captain," Cade pleaded.

"What? With all the bellyaching you've been doing since I 'sentenced' you there, as you put it?"

"I think I may be on to something," Cade said with a shrug of his shoulders. He didn't want to leave Ashleigh unprotected.

"You have something on a possible escort service?" the captain asked.

"No. That was a false lead. I'm working something else. I don't know for sure if it's anything," Cade said evasively, not wanting to overplay his hand if a jealous stripper was behind the threats. "Let me play it out and I'll keep you posted if it turns out to really be something you can use to close the place down."

"Okay," the captain agreed with a show of reluctance when they reached his car. "I can spare you for another week, maybe. But if you don't have anything concrete by then, I'm yanking you back to Homicide, understand?"

"Fair enough," Cade agreed.

The captain got in his car, closed the door and slid down the window. "And one other thing," he called out to Cade who was already walking to where his car was parked a row away. "Keep your hands off the dancers. I don't want to hear anything—"

"Captain, where do you get these ideas that I'm some big Romeo—?"

"In the newspapers, unfortunately," the captain muttered, driving off. The newspapers had had a field day over Cade's involvement with Melodie Fortune.

A gentle rain began to fall as Cade got into his car and headed home, his thoughts on Ashleigh Frost.

He wondered if she'd cooled down by now.

Perhaps he ought to stop by her apartment to see. No, he decided, the captain's warning still fresh in his mind.

Besides, Shadow was home alone.

And he'd been home alone too long. He'd made his displeasure clear in the bathroom. Toilet tissue was everywhere but on the roll.

Still, he'd come when Cade called him, barking, whining, and rolling over on his back to be petted. His wagging tail hit Cade in the face.

"Look what I brought you, boy," Cade said, picking up the sack of leftovers Dave had given him. "Uncle Dave sent you a treat. Next time he comes over you'd better bark nice, and no more hair standing up on your back. It scares people.

They don't know you do it because you're scared of them and you're trying to look bigger."

Shadow wasn't listening. He was too busy chomping down on the special treat.

"You're pretty sad, you know that?" Cade said out loud to himself. "The best relationship you have in your life is with your dog." He shook his head. He supposed it was because he'd grown up fatherless with a mother who worked all the time. A mother who resented him. The joy and devotion he'd experienced in his life had come from a stray dog he'd adopted.

Women were a pleasant diversion, but they came and they went. They all liked the thrill of being with a cop. But most were too smart to want to marry one. They knew the job was dangerous and thankless. One that took a merciless toll on marriages.

Cade walked over to his CD player and put on The Fabulous Thunderbirds. They were just right for his mood.

Slouching down on the black leather sofa, he let the music take him away as Shadow returned to him, nosing his way across his lap like a blanket.

Cade wondered briefly why, when he looked in the mirror, he didn't see the 911 tattooed there that women seemed to notice right away.

How was it he always found a woman who needed rescuing? "Do I look like a knight in shining armor?" he asked aloud, as Shadow gazed up at him.

"Just once I'd like someone to rescue me."

ASHLEIGH SAT at the kitchen counter reading a new magazine she'd subscribed to. It was called *Attitudes*. It had a very saucy viewpoint and she was distracted from her worries by a column called "For the Romantically Challenged." It was written by three romance writers who'd dubbed themselves The Bad Girls' Club. Their advice on love was sassy and audacious.

It had her chuckling and feeling better.

Their philosophy was to take life by the throat and shake it until it coughed up what you wanted. Don't sit around waiting for that phone to ring, for Richard Gere to climb out of a white Cadillac and up your balcony with roses, or for that Publishers Clearing House check to show up in the mail.

You were the only one who could decide who and what you wanted in life, ergo you took charge and got it.

And that was exactly what she needed to do.

She needed to work on building a portfolio she could show to prospective employers. Just sitting around waiting for this part of her life to be over, not living until she'd paid off the debt, was self-indulgent.

Closing the magazine, she went to her art table and sat down. She turned on the swing-arm lamp and studied the drawing she'd left there days ago.

It was of a fingertip-length jacket to go with the nude body stocking she'd designed. Like Donna Karan, she liked clean lines and basic pieces that could be assembled in an individual style by the customer. Except Ashleigh was bored to tears by neutrals.

Pastels—soft pinks, blues and mint greens—were the colors she envisioned for her collection. And she had been adding delicate posies and ribbon closings to suits to soften them.

She picked up her pencil and began sketching.

After finishing the suit, she worked on a drawing of an apron dress, crystallizing an idea she'd had in her mind for some time. When she finished a sketch she was satisfied with, she stopped to flip through a stack of *Women's Wear Daily* newspapers that had accumulated. The suit, she saw, was going to be very big for fall; jackets worn with short skirts or pants, in a wide variety of fabrics.

Satisfied that her designs were unique but on target, she returned to her drawing board and began sketching an innocent-sexy slip dress. As she worked, what she'd been trying to suppress finally surged into her mind.

Cade Hawkins.

What was she going to do about him?

He wanted to protect her.

The problem was, she *wanted* him to.

It would be so easy to fall back on that old habit.

And he was a cop. In other words, a walking marriage disaster. Hadn't she already made enough mistakes in her life?

8

WHEN ASHLEIGH DROVE to the club the following evening she was nervous.

The reasons were manifold: She had with her the new costume she planned to try in her act tonight; the threats someone was making might or might not be harmless, and she was falling for Cade Hawkins, who might or might not be harmless.

Most likely might not be—at least when it came to her independence.

She stopped at Cathy's dressing room to check on her and found her with a well-dressed young woman in an expensive navy business suit.

"Ashleigh, this is Melodie Fortune, the attorney Cade recommended. She's handling my divorce."

Ashleigh shook the woman's hand, finding her grip firm and sure. "I'm happy to meet you, Ms. Fortune." Then she blushed when she realized how the salutation sounded.

Evidently Melodie Fortune had heard it often enough that she didn't react to it any longer.

"Cathy tells me you're the main attraction here, that you are a talented dancer and have a very unusual act. She also tells me you're seeing Cade Hawkins."

"Do you know him?" Ashleigh asked.

"I know him. I'm at the police station a lot because that's where my practice takes me. Cade's a hunky guy, but watch your step with him. Like all the rest of the cops, he's married to his job. Cops don't do well in long-term relationships unless the woman or man involved is willing to understand they come second. Well, so much for my lecture. I think I'll have dinner here tonight and see the show."

"Great, you can see both of our acts," Cathy said happily.

"I need to see Cathy dance because I'm sure her husband will try to use it in the divorce settlement," Melodie explained to Ashleigh. "And I shouldn't feel too conspicuous as Cathy tells me the crowd is becoming more and more mixed, with people on dates as well as singles."

"So then you are going through with the divorce, Cathy?" Ashleigh had not been sure that Cathy would stand firm against her husband.

"No woman should let a man hit her a second time," Melodie declared.

"I certainly agree with that," Ashleigh said, "even though I know how hard it is to face an uncertain future. But I'm finding each day of independence makes me stronger. If the two of you will excuse me, I've got to change," Ashleigh said, taking her leave. She was glad Cathy had reached the decision to leave Dexter Murry, only sorry it had taken a physical blow for her to act. Dexter Murry was bad news just waiting to get on a tabloid cover or TV show.

She was almost afraid to open the door to her dressing room for fear of what she might find. Before the newspaper column she'd been able to dismiss the threats, almost believe she had imagined them. Cade's concerns added to the column's effect, made the threats very real. If he'd meant to scare her, he had succeeded.

She was probably being stubborn and foolish, refusing his protection.

But to her relief, when she went into her dressing room, there were no surprises waiting for her.

Not even Cade Hawkins.

He hadn't been waiting for her outside her apartment. He hadn't struck her as the type of man who'd give up that easily.

She felt stupid for almost being disappointed.

Shrugging off the feeling, she sat down before her dressing table after hanging up her costume and began applying her makeup—to create the face of a woman who could turn on a roomful of men. Was it all illusion or was Ashleigh Frost really that woman?

HER COSTUME HAD BEEN a hit.

She'd played out the fantasy librarian: very sexy black undies beneath a prim-and-proper twinset and pencil-slim skirt.

It had turned the audience on and it had turned her on. Perhaps it was just as well that Cade Hawkins was nowhere to be seen when she left the club.

All work and no play no longer appealed to her. It was time for her to find the love life she'd been missing. But she was clueless about how to go about it. How did women meet men? She couldn't very well meet them at work. Well, she had to amend, she had met Cade there but he seemed to be losing interest.

She was no closer to a solution to her romantic dilemma by the time she arrived home.

Cade Hawkins remained firmly ensconced in her mind, even if physically he had done a disappearing act. Melodie Fortune was right. Cops weren't a good risk for the long term, it appeared.

CADE SAT IN HIS CAR outside Ashleigh's apartment again.

He'd been following her since she'd left there earlier to go to her job at the club, watching to see if anyone else was tailing her.

There hadn't been anyone.

Now that she was safely home, he would go down to the station to run some checks on his list of suspects. As he drove away he switched on the radio station to a late-night talk show, which had Vincent Palmer as its guest. The picketers outside Miss Olivia's might have been ineffectual but that wasn't stopping the restaurant owner from trying to keep the controversy alive.

As Cade listened to Vincent's bitter attack on the club, he came to the conclusion that Miss Olivia's wasn't the only thing Vincent Palmer was trying to suppress.

With the murder rate climbing every day in the metropolitan area, Cade couldn't believe that anyone could get so worked up over women taking off their clothes. Well . . . worked up, yeah, but not in the way Vincent was.

He was fairly certain Vincent had never seen Ashleigh dance. Vincent's concerns had more to do with his wallet. Unfortunately for the restaurateur, when it came to food and sex, most men would choose sex first.

And when it came to Roast Duckling with Blackberry Sauce, Cade would choose sex only. He had a cop's stomach for fast food...and fast women.

That last wasn't really true. He dated fast women because he knew he was unlovable. When your own mother didn't love you... Early on he'd adopted a don't-give-a-damn attitude to cover his longing to be loved. No point in wanting what you couldn't have.

And then Ashleigh had to come along and made him want what he couldn't have.

She was different from the women he usually became involved with. She was innocent. Even if she did take her clothes off in public.

Most important, no one was going to harm her. He might pretend he didn't give a damn, but his actions seemed to prove otherwise.

Cade shook his head. He couldn't believe he was so far gone over a woman he'd only kissed. He blamed J.J. for putting ideas in his head. Ideas about all women not being the same. About there being a special woman who would be foolish enough to marry a cop because she loved him. A woman like what J.J. had found in Monica.

Maybe a woman like Ashleigh.

Yeah, right.

HE'D BEEN AT THE POLICE station about ten minutes when the call came in.

It was Ashleigh and she needed him.

He got to her apartment in half the time it had taken him to drive from her place to the station.

When he knocked on her door, her shaky voice asked, "Who is it?"

"It's the police," Cade answered. "Open up, Ashleigh. It's me, Cade."

She unlocked the door and let him in.

"What is it? What's wrong?" he asked.

On the phone when she'd called him for help she'd been crying and too upset to talk.

"In my bedroom..." She led the way and Cade followed.

Her closet door was open. The clothes were destroyed. Someone had ripped and shredded them with a knife. Everything hung in tatters.

"Why...why would someone do this?" she whispered, still shocked over what she'd found when she'd been getting ready to go to bed.

"Does anyone else have a key to your apartment?" Cade demanded, the cop in him taking over.

She shook her head no.

"Are you okay?" he asked.

"Yes, I'm just upset. Nothing like this has ever happened to me before. I thought the notes were harmless, but this is really scary," she sniffed. "Someone hates me."

"No. Someone hates himself and is taking it out on you. Someone wants to scare you."

"It's working," Ashleigh said, trembling.

"You're going to be all right," Cade assured her, afraid she might jump if he hugged her.

After checking out the doors and windows and finding no sign of forced entry, Cade returned to where a despondent Ashleigh sat on her bed. "Do you leave your keys in your dressing room when you dance?"

She just looked at him.

"Of course, you do. As I recall there wasn't a pocket for your keys in your costume. I'm guessing someone slipped into your dressing room while you were onstage."

"But I keep my door locked, ever since the—"

"Those dressing-room doors would open with a credit card slipped into the doorframe."

Ashleigh's face was pale. "You're telling me that someone can come into my apartment whenever they please?"

"No, the first thing we're going to do is have your locks changed in the morning. And until morning, you're coming home with me."

"I'm what?"

"I've got a spare bedroom you can have all to yourself. I want you where I can protect you."

"Then why not sleep here on my sofa . . . ?"

"Because I've got a dog who doesn't like to spend the night alone."

"You're making that all up, right?" Ashleigh asked, smiling for the first time since she'd found the ruined clothing.

Cade shook his head, looking sorrowful. "Unfortunately, no. The last time I came home really late, he'd papered my bathroom and the hall. He would have papered the whole house but he ran out of toilet paper. So far, he hasn't figured out how to open drawers and doors to get more. But if I stay out all night, there is no telling what he might do. Come to think of it, I've seen him drooling over my leather sofa when he didn't know I was looking. He just might start using it for a great big chew toy."

"Okay, you've intrigued me," Ashleigh said, giving in, her earlier fear subsiding with Cade's gentle humor.

"Then throw a few things in a bag and we'll get out of here. I'll have the guys come over in the morning to dust for prints. If we get lucky, maybe we'll learn who's so determined to scare off Miss Olivia's main attraction."

Ashleigh did as he requested. She avoided looking into her closet as she tossed what she'd need for the night into a flowered carryall. Whether it was a smart move or not, she felt much better when she left with Cade.

He switched the radio station in his car the minute they got in, finding an oldies station playing Motown. He didn't want some talk show upsetting Ashleigh.

"You like oldies?" she inquired.

"From the fifties and sixties. Otherwise I like blues. How about you?"

"Me too. I mean blues. I really like Eric Clapton, do you?"

"Eric's the man. But I'm particularly fond of The Fabulous Thunderbirds. Have you heard any of the local blues bands?" He thought it wasn't the right time to ask if she'd like to go see one with him sometime. He managed not to ask her.

"They've got some great ones—Patty and the Hit Men, No Exit Blues Band, Soulard Blues Band . . ."

"And there's this girl who plays a wailing sax—"

"Sydney something, isn't it?"

"Yeah, I think it is. So you like blues, then."

She nodded. "Yeah. Somehow, listening to it makes me feel better."

"I know what you mean."

The rest of the ride was in silence as both of them suddenly felt shy with each other after the rush of shared passion, if only for a kind of music.

When he pulled into the drive, Ashleigh had fallen asleep. He parked and nudged her shoulder gently, waking her.

"We're here," he announced.

As they walked up to the front door he wondered how Shadow was going to react.

He'd never brought a woman home with him before.

SHADOW HAD DONE a lot better than him.

Shadow had slept with Ashleigh.

While Cade hadn't slept at all.

But despite his lack of sleep he felt wonderful, full of energy. He'd gone for his run alone, Shadow not even lifting his head when Cade had peeked in on the two. The only thing that had brought Shadow to his side was the smell of breakfast cooking. Now the silly dog followed him around the kitchen so that Cade was tripping over him every time he turned around.

He'd called Monica and woken her to get the recipe for her egg-and-sausage breakfast casserole that he loved. After his run he'd picked up the ingredients along with fresh croissants and a sack of oranges.

Shadow could smell the casserole cooking and kept nudging Cade with his nose, begging for some.

Cade checked the oven. It was almost ready.

"Go wake Ashleigh, if you want to eat," Cade ordered Shadow.

Shadow cocked his head and looked at Cade.

"Go on, go fetch the pretty lady."

Shadow whined, his tail wagging. "Yeah, I know how you feel," Cade said, finishing up the fresh oranges he was squeezing for juice. "I like her, too."

Shadow scampered off, clicking down the hall.

It was odd, Cade thought, having someone besides Shadow sleeping at his place. While Shadow had made the place less lonely, a woman made it warmer. A woman made it seem like a home.

Even a sleeping woman.

He took the sausage-and-egg casserole out of the oven and set it on a rack to cool a little. Then, after pouring the fresh-squeezed orange juice into a pitcher, he placed it in the refrigerator and went to see if Shadow needed any help.

"Good morning," Cade said, sticking his head in the spare bedroom, jealous of Shadow who was licking Ashleigh awake.

Ashleigh giggled and hugged the big dog. Then she smiled at Cade and his stomach fell. He was gone. All she had to do was reel him in.

Only she didn't even know she'd hooked him.

"Breakfast is ready," he said, then left the room before he made a fool of himself.

Cade brushed a lock of hair, still damp from his shower, from his forehead, trying not to think about the woman who had him wanting to make promises about "forevermore." She'd think he was a head case. They barely knew each other.

Maybe they'd get better acquainted over breakfast.

He heard the shower running and his mind got better acquainted with the image of her naked body, slick with white soapsuds. Of her hands moving over her body where he imagined his touching. Where his mouth— Damn!

He looked down to see the source of the sudden sharp, hot stab of pain he'd felt. While slicing the croissants he'd sliced his thumb. He tossed down the knife and grabbed a paper towel to stanch the flow of blood, swearing all the while at his foolishness.

For heaven's sake, he wasn't some teenage boy. Even if he was acting like it.

He needed gauze and adhesive tape to bandage the deep cut, but they were in the bathroom where Ashleigh was showering. Perhaps he could sneak in and grab some from the medicine cabinet without her knowing. Listening, he heard the shower still running.

Shadow lay outside the door, waiting for Ashleigh to come out.

Cade lifted his finger to his lips to shush Shadow while trying the lock on the bathroom door. He was in luck; it was unlocked.

While the water still thundered from the shower, Cade eased open the door to be met with a wall of foggy steam. A quick glance at the shower door told him Ashleigh couldn't see him because she was bent forward with her hair flowing under the shower as she washed it. Quickly, he slid open the medicine cabinet, found the tape and gauze, and removed it.

He was a cop, not a saint, so he sneaked a lingering look at Ashleigh's image—her breasts taut, with water sluicing from them. As he slipped from the bathroom, closing the door behind him and nearly tripping over Shadow, his thumb wasn't the only thing that was throbbing.

In the kitchen he concentrated on bandaging his thumb one handedly. Luckily the thumb he'd cut was his left one so it was a manageable task, at least.

By the time Ashleigh had dressed and come out to the kitchen, he was almost back to normal.

"You certainly know how to get a woman roused," she said, sniffing the aromas in the air—a mixture of sage and citrus.

"What?"

"The smell of hot breakfast will do it every time," Ashleigh explained, nodding at the breakfast casserole on the countertop.

"Oh." For a moment there, he thought she'd said "*a*roused."

"Have a seat at the table. It's all ready," he said, turning away.

"What happened to your thumb!" she asked, seeing the pristine white bandage when he brought the casserole to the table.

He made light of it, laughing. "I'm afraid I'm more of a novice in the kitchen than I'd wanted you to believe."

Shadow barked, wanting the breakfast he'd been so patiently waiting for. "Okay, boy. I'll give you a plate, if you behave. Go lie down."

Cade made good on his word and after giving a plate to Shadow returned to the table with the pitcher of fresh orange juice and a plate of croissants he'd warmed in the toaster oven.

"You may be a novice, but I'm impressed," Ashleigh said, biting into a forkful of casserole from her plate. "Where'd you learn to cook like this?"

"It's Monica's recipe. I got it from her this morning when I called J.J. to check if the guys found anything when they dusted your place for prints."

"Did they find anything?" she asked, pouring a glass of orange juice.

Cade shook his head no. "Just your prints."

"You don't think I'm doing it—"

"Of course not." He passed her the plate of croissants. "Here, try the croissants I slaved so hard over," he said with a grin.

She took one, then asked about a locksmith—if he knew one to recommend.

"I've already taken care of it," Cade replied, tucking into the mound of breakfast casserole on his plate. "They did it first thing this morning."

Shadow was back, his nose poking at Cade's hand.

"You'll have to forgive my dog. I'm pretty lax about table manners since I never have company."

"Where'd you get him? He's a real sweetheart."

"He got me. Flunked out of the police academy and I sort of inherited him when no one else wanted a dog that was afraid of its own shadow."

"Oh, so that's where he got his name."

Cade nodded, swallowing. "He sure does like you."

"The feeling is mutual. I've never had a dog. My parents said they were too much trouble and my ex-husband just said no."

Cade smiled. "And you listened?"

"I used to until I figured out that when someone tells you something is what's best for you, the truth is it's what's best for them."

Unsaid between them was how that figured in Cade's urging her to come home with him.

"Where is your ex-husband, anyway?" Cade asked, curious about why she never spoke of him. She didn't seem to have the bitterness one might expect, given what he'd dumped on her.

"I don't know." Ashleigh shrugged, her wet hair she'd pulled up in a ponytail swinging as she did so. "He just disappeared once I divorced him and left the creditors to feed on me."

"My dad did the same thing to my mom when I was about two," Cade confessed. "It goes without saying what I think about men who act like boys when it comes to the hard parts of life. I see them every day on the streets. Young men who have the power to make life and to take life, but not the balls to live it. Sorry," he apologized. "Guess the language creeps in, when you spend so much time in the streets."

"But you've been spending a lot of time at the club," Ashleigh countered.

"That's because I'm being punished."

"For what?"

"Let's just say I wasn't thinking straight at the time and I let my personal life infringe upon my job." He polished off the last of his breakfast and pushed back his plate.

"You mean like now?" Ashleigh asked pointedly.

"Well . . ."

"You always bring home women who've been victimized by burglars?"

"No, you're the first," he said.

Ashleigh pushed her plate away, as well. She braced her elbows on the table and her chin on her folded hands, looking at him. "So why me, Cade?" she asked searchingly, putting him directly on the spot.

He could dodge her question.

He could answer it.

Either way, he was in trouble.

He decided to try to answer it honestly. For himself as well as for her. "You believe in love at first sight?" he asked.

"You mean lust at first sight. . . ."

He shook his head.

"No, I mean love. For lust I wouldn't have needed to bring you home with me. I could have had you right there in your apartment."

"Does this confidence come with the gun and the badge?" she challenged.

"No. What I meant was you were vulnerable. I could have pushed the situation and coaxed you into wanting me to hold you."

"You wouldn't have had to coax," Ashleigh informed him, baldly honest.

"And now?" he asked, leaning toward her.

She smiled, pulling back. "I'm rested, showered, fed, and much stronger."

"And I'm an idiot."

"No. You're a nice guy."

"I've heard about them—they finish last."

"Not in the nineties."

The flirting was over, the time had passed. They were back to being friends. He was an idiot. But once he'd solved who was behind the threats to Ashleigh, they were going to tangle—between the sheets.

And in life.

"Let's get you back to your apartment and I'll get back to investigating."

"Okay, but first let me do the dishes since you made breakfast," Ashleigh offered, picking up the dirty plates from the table.

"I know a good deal when I see one, so you won't get any argument from me. Besides, I need to exercise Shadow with a quick game of Frisbee before we head out. Then he'll be content to sleep on the couch or watch the birds and squirrels by the feeder until I return.

"Come on, boy," Cade said, picking up the soft Frisbee on the floor by the sofa and leading the dog outside to play in the front yard.

Ashleigh watched from the window over the sink as she did the breakfast dishes.

The scene was domestic.

A fantasy.

Cade was all masculine dark grace as he ran, jumped, fell and played with Shadow. The love between man and dog was uninhibited.

They were hers.

Another fantasy.

The reality—Cade Hawkins had brought her home. It meant nothing. He was a cop with a soft spot for women in distress.

And yet she couldn't look away.

She stood at the window watching him; the way he stood with his wrists bent on his hips, waiting for Shadow to trot back and drop the Frisbee he'd retrieved at Cade's feet, the way he flashed his smile when Shadow twirled in the air and snagged the Frisbee, and the way he tossed back the lock of hair that kept falling on his face with a thrust of his hand.

Her mind was taking snapshots, betraying her by putting them in an album it would take out and flip through at will, tormenting her with what she wanted.

Tormenting her with what she didn't have.

For she knew that yes, she could "coax" Cade Hawkins into bed.

But what she also knew was that, unlike when her ex-husband left, she couldn't bear it when Cade had gone.

Only a foolish woman would give her heart to a cop.

The dangerous job took a heavy toll on marriages.

And lives.

He could be dead at the pull of a druggie's trigger, in the blink of an eye. And how would she ever survive that?

9

CADE BEGAN ESCORTING Ashleigh to work from her apartment. And driving her home. He thought she liked having him around, but she wouldn't let him inside her apartment. He couldn't figure out why. He was a nice guy.

Every night he'd coax.

"Come on . . . let me in."

"No." The no was firm, unwavering.

"Please, pretty please," he'd tease. But to no avail.

"I let you sleep over at my house," he countered.

"My home is my castle. No one but me gets to come in." What she didn't tell him was that the moat was around her heart.

"You're a tough woman, Ashleigh Frost."

"You're the one who told me a woman can't be too careful, Cade." She'd actually thrown his own words back at him.

"You aren't scared of *me*—"

"No, of me."

Saturday night was different, however.

Saturday night the picketers weren't outside Miss Olivia's. Although Harry Wolfe was there, his column "Prowling the Night" hadn't mentioned the club for several days. There hadn't been any more threats.

And Cade was out of time.

He didn't have answers for his captain and his week was up.

Cade was quiet as he waited for Ashleigh to perform onstage. He noticed Cathy was in a good mood. The bruise on her cheek had healed and she and Tommy Gardner were getting chummy.

Ashleigh's performance followed Cathy's. The usual din of the club ebbed away as the crowd watched, transfixed, while Ashleigh performed her librarian fantasy. Cade enjoyed it all to hell—which was where not touching her kept him.

The club was closed on Sunday and so when Cade drove Ashleigh home, the tension between them relaxed. He was wondering how he was going to tell her that he would no longer be able to protect her while he was on duty.

Parking the car, he took a bouquet of red roses from the trunk and presented her with them. As it happened he'd wasted his money. He hadn't needed them to advance his romance.

She squealed with delight, so he stood there beside the car smiling at her and feeling sheepish while she smelled the bouquet.

But then she was crying, fat teardrops sliding down her cheeks. She was glad she'd decided to chance lowering the drawbridge over the moat . . . risking her heart.

"What's wrong?" he asked, all concern.

"No one has ever given me roses before."

"I guess that's my cue to be going," he said, wiping a tear from her damp cheek with his bandaged thumb.

"*No*. No, I want you to come in tonight."

"You do?"

She nodded. "I'll make you a new bandage for your thumb. That one is getting pretty shabby."

"Thanks, nurse."

But they didn't make it to the medicine cabinet straight away.

Or to the kitchen for a vase for the flowers.

The roses scattered to the floor around them when he pulled her into his arms, sweeping her into a passionate, romantic kiss.

"Just slap me if I'm out of line," Cade said, knowing full well by her response that he wasn't.

She still wore the librarian outfit; had worn it purposely.

She felt prim and improper.

Sexy.

She didn't slap him. Instead she cupped his face with her hands and pulled his lips back to hers in an inviting kiss. Seductive. Sweet.

He didn't have to be asked twice.

His lips played at hers, teasing, toying. And all the while her pulse was racing wildly.

She closed her eyes, enjoying the smell of his modern cologne mixed with the scent of roses drifting up from the floor.

And then the scent of roses was stronger as they slid to the floor. Somewhere in a heartbeat the seduction had escalated into full-blown passion.

He was groaning, she was moaning, both were breathing in shallow gasps.

"I want you like hell," Cade voiced, making sure he wasn't misunderstanding the signals she gave off.

"Is it the costume?" she asked, only half kidding.

"I don't think so. I've been wanting you like hell since the first moment I laid eyes on you. How about you? Do you want me?"

"Yes."

"Is it the costume?" he asked, only half kidding.

"What?"

"Is it the badge and the gun? Is it because I'm a cop?"

"No. It's in spite of your being a cop."

"You're turning into a risk junkie, are you?" he asked, taking her hand and placing it on the steel-hard bulge straining at his fly.

"No, I'm turning into a Cade Hawkins junkie," she replied, laughing, the sound sexy and provocative—strange to her ears. She could taste him on her lips. A hint of the cinnamon gum he sometimes chewed mingled with the essence of him. It was like a drug to her senses, making her tremble.

His hand slid swiftly beneath her skirt, past the lacy tops of the black stockings to her panties. He slipped his fingertips beneath the flutter of her lettice-edged tap pants and stroked her moist, hot sex. There was no nude bodysuit as there had been onstage. She wanted him. She wanted *him*. If he could make her want him, then maybe he could make her love him.

"You want me as much as I want you. Say it."

"I want you. Please, Cade."

She could feel his chest rising and falling as she began unbuttoning his shirt to pull it free from his pants. His own hands had left her briefly to undo the buckle of his belt. Pulling his belt free, he discarded it.

She had his shirt undone and reached for his zipper.

"You'd better let me do that," he said, staying her hand and carefully freeing his desire for her, to her hand.

"You're satiny hard for me, Cade. I want to feel you inside me. Now, Cade."

Without a single word, without a single wasted movement, he granted her request.

Pushing aside her tap pants, he entered her with a sure thrust. His hands gripped hers and he braced himself on his elbows as he continued thrusting, slowly and deeply and then withdrawing.

His neck was arched and her head was thrashing from side to side as both fought to catch their breath and ride the wave of passionate desire that swept them ever further until he cried out with one last, deep thrust. She felt him throb inside her, and hugged him hard, biting his neck and moaning.

When she finally opened her eyes, his were looking straight into hers.

He smiled, evidently satisfied with what he read there.

She returned his satisfied smile.

He rolled to one side then, and gave out a bloody yell, "Ouch!"

"What is it?" she asked, alarmed.

He rolled forward, reaching behind him to pick up a long-stemmed red rose; the thorn had dug into his skin.

"Sorry," Ashleigh apologized. "I guess I should have stopped to put them in water."

"Like I'd have let you. Besides, this is more romantic—no pain, no gain."

He began gathering up the roses, though, until he held the bouquet in his hand.

"Do you want me to find a vase?" Ashleigh asked, sitting up.

"No. I want you to stay put. I've got an idea."

She watched as he began making a bed of rose petals on the carpet with the bouquet, holding only stems in his hands when he had finished with the task he'd set for himself.

Grinning, he tossed the stems away and reached for her.

"What are you going to do?"

"One way or another, I'm going to make you blush," he vowed.

And he did.

ASHLEIGH'S SCREAM made Cade sit upright out of a dead sleep.

She stood just inside the doorway of her bedroom and he reached her in three strides.

"What is it?" he demanded, throwing his arms around her to calm her.

"There," she pointed at the white cheval mirror in the corner of the bedroom.

Someone had scrawled a message on it in blood-red lipstick.

I WARNED YOU, BUT IT'S
TOO LATE TO GET OUT NOW.

"When?" Cade asked.

"I don't know. It wasn't there when I left for work last night. It could have been there when we came back here last night. We . . . I . . . didn't come into the bedroom until just now."

She turned her face into his chest and began sobbing.

It was a nightmare.

"It's going to be all right," he promised her. "I'm going to find out who's doing this and why. And they aren't going to frighten you ever again."

His assurances didn't help.

It was too much.

It made his skin crawl, too.

He held her until the police arrived to check out the scene.

There was no sign of forced entry.

There was no clue left behind other than the tube of red lipstick that had been dropped on the carpet—a ruined mess.

"That settles it. You're coming to stay with me until this is solved," Cade instructed.

"No."

"Ashleigh, don't be foolish."

"No."

He played dirty. "Shadow will be all alone if I have to stay here every night."

She went with him.

WHOEVER HAD LEFT the message scrawled on her mirror had gotten what they wanted.

Ashleigh gave Tommy Gardner her notice the next morning over his vigorous objections.

He offered her a raise, a new dressing room, whatever she wanted.

But nothing worked.

She'd made up her mind.

It would be better to declare bankruptcy than to continue living with the fear that was now a part of her life she couldn't shake.

Anymore than she could shake Cade Hawkins.

Even if she wanted to.

10

ASHLEIGH WAS nervous.

J.J. and his wife were coming for dinner and she had cooked. It was the least she could do after Cade had been so wonderful to her. He'd taken a few days of vacation just to be with her to help her get over the trauma of being stalked. She didn't know how she would have coped without him.

And now tonight J.J. was coming over to bring them up to date on what, if anything, the police had been able to discover about who had been threatening her.

She wanted to make a good impression on Cade's friends. First because of Cade, and second, because she'd really liked them when they'd come back to meet her after her performance at Miss Olivia's. She was looking forward to talking with Monica about fashion.

Cade was in the shower getting ready while she put the finishing touches to the meal of baked ham, spaghetti and spinach salad. She'd made her special dressing for the spinach salad in the blender, one of the few decent kitchen appliances Cade had.

The kitchen was still a little steamy from the pasta she'd boiled, but she'd transferred it and the rich sauce to the Crock-Pot to keep the spaghetti warm until the dinner guests arrived. Pulling the ham out, she basted it once more.

The mixing of the spinach salad could wait till just before they were ready to eat. She'd already assembled the other ingredients—sliced hard-boiled eggs, crumbled bacon, sprouts, and mushrooms and Bermuda onions sliced thin.

With a quick glance at the table she'd already set, Ashleigh slipped off her white apron just as the doorbell rang.

"Could you get it, Ashleigh? I'm not ready yet," Cade called out.

Ashleigh answered the door and ushered J.J. and his wife inside just as Cade came down the hall dressed, but barefoot, his shoes in one hand.

"Sorry, I'm running late. Shadow saw a squirrel when I took him out for a walk and ran after the critter for three miles. But at least he's worn-out. He's sound asleep on my bed."

"Good, then he won't be in my lap during dinner," J.J. said, handing Ashleigh a bottle of Stone Hill white Rhine wine from the Missouri winery.

"O-h-h-h...sexy!" Cade teased J.J., fingering his friend's new suede vest backed with a paisley twill. "You win this in a poker game?"

"Knock it off, Cade," Monica said, used to Cade teasing J.J. about her fashion finds for her husband. "I don't think anyone's interested in the opinion of someone who greets his guests barefoot."

"Touché," Cade agreed affably.

"What smells so good? Can't be anything you cooked, Cade," J.J. said as they entered the living room.

"You're right. Ashleigh cooked."

"Sounds like you're a woman of many talents," Monica observed.

"Do you cook?" Ashleigh asked.

At the question, both J.J. and Cade broke up into gales of laughter.

"What they're trying to tell you in their oh-so-subtle way, Ashleigh," Monica said, shooting both men a jaundiced look, "is that the only thing I know how to make is reservations."

"Oh." Ashleigh didn't know what to say to that.

Cade finally had his shoes on and suggested they eat.

Monica and J.J. sat down at the table.

They exchanged knowing looks as Ashleigh and Cade lingered in the kitchen. "Think I should go out there and throw some cold water on them, or something?" J.J. whispered.

"I think you should behave," Monica whispered back as the two rejoined them, carrying food.

When they sat down Cade nuzzled the back of Ashleigh's neck, whispering something wicked that made her blush.

"I don't care what you say, I'm getting water and—"

"Sit down," Monica said, pulling J.J. back to his chair and kicking him under the table.

"He wants to put catsup on everything," Monica said, by way of explanation.

Ashleigh accepted the compliments on the meal and in turn complimented Monica on her outfit, a sophisticated, tailored coatdress in an above-the-knee length with a tieback that accentuated Monica's tiny waist.

"I've been thinking," Monica said, "since Cade told me you plan to be a designer, that maybe I could help you. I have a lot of contacts in the fashion business. Do you have a portfolio I could show around for you?"

"You'd do that?"

"Why, sure."

"My designs are at my apartment. I could get them for you, I suppose."

"Tell you what, why don't I meet you at your apartment tomorrow about five to pick them up?

I'm flying out of town tomorrow night, so I'd want to have them with me to look over."

"Okay. Thanks, Monica."

Ashleigh wanted to pinch herself. She couldn't believe she was in Cade's home, having dinner with Cade's friends and having them offer to help her, just as Cade had. Her luck had definitely gotten better.

But it couldn't continue.

Couldn't last.

She couldn't get involved seriously with anyone until she'd settled the debt her ex-husband had left her with. And getting involved with a cop was dicey at best. She had to be sensible and make a wise choice about what to do with her life, not act on lust.

Perhaps not even act on love . . .

"So tell us what you've found out so far about the second break-in at Ashleigh's apartment," Cade said, taking another helping of spinach salad.

J.J. put down his fork and swallowed the last of the mound of spaghetti on his plate before answering. "I'm afraid we've got zip."

"Nothing?" Cade said with disbelief.

"That's about the size of it."

"Still no sign of forced entry—"

"Nope."

"Then how did . . . ?"

"We don't know. Someone had to have had a key to get into the apartment."

"But I just had the locks changed," Ashleigh said, the fear returning.

"I know," J.J. agreed. "It just doesn't make sense. Unless . . ."

"I guess someone could make a copy of your key by making an impression if you left it lying around somewhere."

"What about the lipstick?" Cade interjected.

J.J. shook his head negatively.

"Both lipsticks belonged to Ashleigh. Neither tube had any distinguishable prints on them. Evidently whoever it was just picked up whatever was handy to scribble what was on their mind."

"What about suspects?" Cade interjected.

"Surely it's just some nutcase," Monica said, taking a sip of her wine.

"Maybe," Cade agreed. "But maybe not."

"Well, we know the club manager appears to be clean. Harry Wolfe is making hay with this latest incident in his column. Dexter Murry hasn't been seen around the club since Cathy filed for divorce."

"What about Cathy?" J.J. asked.

"Surely you don't suspect—" Ashleigh asked.

"I suspect everybody."

"Well, since Ashleigh quit, Cathy has become the featured performer at Miss Olivia's and she and Tommy Gardner are quite an item, so the gossip goes."

"That would mean the threats would stop if it was her and she got what she wanted, right?" Monica said.

"That's right, babe," J.J. answered. "And here all this time I didn't think you listened when I talked shop."

"Of course, I listen." Monica winked at Ashleigh.

"What about Vincent Palmer?" J.J. offered. "Any more on him or do you think he's given up?"

"Well, he certainly hasn't gotten what he wanted," Cade said. "I wouldn't bet on him giving up on anything. He's got the look of a fanatic in his eyes. But if it is Vincent, then there's no reason for him to threaten Ashleigh any longer since she's no longer working at Miss Olivia's. He'll have to terrorize someone else, and give himself away in the doing."

"Have you come up with anything on Ashleigh's ex-husband?" Cade asked.

"Cade! Surely you don't think—"

"Everyone is a suspect, Ashleigh. If he'd leave you with a pile of his debts, he'd do anything. Maybe he got wind of your success and was jealous of it. Who knows what goes on in people's minds these days?"

"That's the truth," J.J. agreed.

"How long were you married?" Monica asked Ashleigh. "You barely look out of your teens."

"I'm *not* robbing the cradle, Monica," Cade insisted.

"I'm twenty-one," Ashleigh replied. "And I was married for a year."

"You are too robbing the cradle," Monica admonished Cade. But then she smiled at Ashleigh and said, "But I can't say as I blame you. Finally you find a woman with some style. It's about time, even if you had to go to the local high school to do it." She winked at Ashleigh so she wouldn't take offense.

"We haven't turned up anything on him," J.J. said, answering Cade's question about Ashleigh's ex-husband. "He seems to have truly disappeared. I'd guess he's left the area."

"And I say we don't talk shop anymore," Monica declared. "Didn't someone say something about a chocolate cheesecake for dessert?"

"THANK YOU," Ashleigh said, when she'd finished the dishes with Cade drying. "I had a good time tonight with J.J. and Monica. Although J.J. has a killer instinct when it comes to charades."

"That's because you women cheated, using chick movie titles we've never heard of."

"Yeah, but we won," Ashleigh said on a smile.

"Maybe I'm a sore loser and I plan to exact payment for the humiliation of losing to a couple of women," Cade proposed, pulling her into his arms.

"Maybe I'll let you," Ashleigh replied, giggling when he began kissing her neck where she was ticklish.

"But on one condition," she said, pulling away.

"What's that?"

"No carpet burns . . ."

"You got it. I'll carry you to my soft bed and make wild passionate love to you until you beg me to stop." With that, Cade swept her up into his arms.

"How much wine have you had to drink?" Ashleigh asked with a giggle.

"Not that much. See, I can walk a straight line." He demonstrated, carrying her down the hall.

"Yeah, when you want to. But how often do you choose that path?"

"Since I met you?" he ventured.

"Right answer. Score two points."

"Does that mean I get to pass Go?"

"If you can manage to stay out of jail . . ."

"Oh, I don't know. . . . I've got these handcuffs that are just lying around collecting dust. Maybe—"

"Forget it. You'd never be able to operate the key and I'd have to explain to J.J.—"

"Yeah, forget it. He'd never let me live that one down," Cade agreed.

"So just some good old-fashioned lovemaking, then?" Cade asked, kicking open the bedroom door with his foot.

"With a nineties twist," Ashleigh said.

"A nineties twist? That sounds interesting. What's a nineties twist?"

"I get to be on top. I'm afraid with the wine for dinner, a full stomach and your long walk with Shadow that you may fall asleep during."

"What! I've never fallen asleep during. I don't even fall asleep after. And you've got the rug burns to prove it," Cade said, affronted.

"Cade?"

"Hmm..."

"I think it's a moot point."

"Why?"

Ashleigh pointed to where one hundred pounds of German shepherd lay sprawled diagonally across the bed, snoring.

"Morning sex is good," Cade offered hopefully.

11

THE MORNING SEX had been delicious.

Cade had gone off to the police station with a smile on his face and a hickey on his neck . . . and some of Ashleigh's concealer on it.

She hadn't told him, but when she'd hugged him goodbye she'd rubbed the concealer off on purpose.

J.J. was going to have a blast.

While she was showering, Ashleigh came up with an idea for another item to add to her portfolio. She made plans to go to the store and pick up some sketching paper while taking Shadow to the vet for his annual rabies shot.

She couldn't let herself hope too much that Monica might be able to put her in touch with a job lead because the disappointment would be overwhelming if it didn't come true.

But she did have hopes.

By three o'clock that afternoon Ashleigh had finished her errands and sketched until she had a good illustration of the new lace-edged camp shirt and boxer shorts for her portfolio.

Leaving Shadow with a rawhide treat she'd bought him, she headed to her apartment to meet Monica at five as they had arranged. She'd left early because she didn't want to be late, didn't want anything to mess up this chance Monica was giving her.

She hadn't counted on how uneasy she would feel when she got to the apartment. The last time she'd been there, there was a threat scrawled on her bedroom mirror.

But there hadn't been any warnings since then. And she was firmly convinced the threats had to do with her working at Miss Olivia's. So she opened the door to her apartment and went inside, telling herself that everything was all right in her life now. Cade was in her life.

Someone had washed the lipsticked words off the mirror and that helped. After a quick search she located her portfolio. Someone had moved it into the closet. It had been sitting out when the police had come.

Taking her portfolio of designs to the living room, she sat down to look through it, flipping on the television to keep her company. A talk show was on with people yelling at each other, but she tuned it out, becoming immersed in her sketches, trying to study them with a dispassionate eye.

The ringing of the doorbell made her jump. She'd become lost in what she was doing and hadn't realized how much time had passed.

Could it be five o'clock already? She glanced down at her watch. It was only four.

Perhaps Monica had gotten the time mixed up or her flight out of town had been moved to an earlier departure time.

Setting her portfolio aside, Ashleigh got up from her chair and went to answer the door. To her surprise, it was Cathy.

"You're here. I've been trying to catch you for days."

"Why? Is something wrong? Did Dexter—"

"No. He's being surprisingly decent about the divorce. My attorney says he's a wuss. That most men who hit women are, when confronted by someone strong."

"I overheard J.J. saying something about Melodie Fortune being a man-eater. But I guess when you're good in a man's world there is bound to be some resentment." Ashleigh stepped back and invited Cathy into the apartment.

"So why have you come by?" Ashleigh smiled. "Do you have some magic you want to show me? I hear you're the lead dancer now at Miss Olivia's."

"That's what I came to talk to you about," Cathy said, walking past Ashleigh.

"Can I get you something to drink? I think there might be a soda or something in the refrigerator," Ashleigh offered, going to look.

"No. I don't want anything," Cathy replied. "And will you stop being so damn nice to me!"

At Cathy's harsh words, Ashleigh spun around to face her.

"I came here to ask if you were planning to come back to dance at Miss Olivia's," Cathy said. "Or if you'd really decided to quit like Tommy said you have."

"I'm not coming back," Ashleigh confirmed.

"I see." Cathy bit her bottom lip.

"Cathy, what's wrong?"

"I'm what's wrong," Cathy muttered, not meeting Ashleigh's gaze. "Do you remember when Tommy called us all into his office and told us about Harry Wolfe's column and the threatening notes someone had been receiving?"

Ashleigh nodded, watching Cathy warily since she was acting strange.

"Just before that, Dexter had made fun of me. Made fun of the magic you suggested I put in my act. He said that you only wanted me to look dumb. That you didn't want anyone competing with you. I thought he was right."

"Are you trying to tell me that you were jealous of me? That you let Dexter poison you against me?"

"It's true."

"You're the one who—"

"I'm the one who broke into your apartment and ripped up your clothes."

"How . . . how did you get in?" Ashleigh asked, stalling for time—uncertain what Cathy might do, and why she was there telling her what she'd done.

"It was easy. I just used a credit card. I notice you changed the lock."

"You threatened me because you weren't the lead dancer, Cathy? I can't believe it."

"I can't either," Cathy said, beginning to cry. "I—"

"Those threats, the note and the messages scrawled with my own lipstick. How could you scare me like that, Cathy? I thought we were friends!"

"I only ripped your clothes. I'm not the one who sent the threatening messages. They only gave me the idea. I was sorry as soon as I'd done it, but I couldn't confess because I was afraid the police would arrest me. But now that you're safe—I mean, you're living with a cop and all—I thought maybe you could find it in your heart to forgive what I did. I'll repay you for the damage to your clothes. I promise. Please, Ashleigh. I am so sorry."

Cathy broke down in tears and Ashleigh didn't have the heart not to forgive her.

She put her arms around Cathy and hugged her until she stopped crying.

"Do you promise not to tell anyone?" Cathy asked. "I feel like such a fool. I don't know what came over me. I guess Dexter made me feel so insecure and I was afraid of losing him. Once I'd decided I was going to lose him anyway, I realized what a fool I'd been all this time."

"I promise," Ashleigh agreed. After all, she'd been a fool, too. She knew what it felt like. Cathy's act had been an isolated incident, not like the planned series of threats to scare her.

When Cathy was gone, Ashleigh went to look for the costume she'd been working on before everything had gone crazy. She found it in the top of her closet and was just getting it down when the doorbell rang again.

This time it was Monica.

"These designs are fabulous," Monica said when they were sprawled on the carpet with Ashleigh's portfolio.

"There's glamour *and* comfort in your designs. And the mood is romantic, which I think is right for the last half of the nineties."

"You really like them?" Ashleigh asked, her voice breathy with excitement. She couldn't believe someone with Monica's knowledge of fashion really liked her work. It was a dream come true.

"Like them? I love them. And I'm going to find a place for you."

"Are you . . . I mean, I can't believe . . ."

"You have an artist's eye for mixing colors. I want to be the one who discovered you. These jackets are wonderful smudgy-smoky neutrals. I want one."

"You've got one," Ashleigh promised.

"Have you thought about designing for men?" Monica asked, studying one of her illustrations of a dressing-gown evening jacket.

"I'm not sure I could."

"Try it. I'll order a custom evening jacket for J.J. from you. Surprise me."

J.J. must love Monica very much, Ashleigh thought, to withstand all the grief his fellow cops gave him over the clothing choices she made for him.

Somehow Monica got up from the floor gracefully in her gravity-defying miniskirt and took the portfolio Ashleigh had reshuffled back together.

"Take good care of the boys while I'm gone," Monica said as she left. "Neither of them should be allowed out on their own, much less together. I'm so pleased Cade has found someone at last who will really care for him. He needs caring for, though he never shows it.

"Women have come so easily to him because of his great good looks, but love—that hasn't come at all.

"Until now."

"I don't—"

"I do," Monica assured her.

When she was gone Ashleigh almost burst into dance she was so happy.

Happy because Monica had liked her designs.

Happy because she felt confident the people Monica knew would like her designs, too.

And happier still, because Monica believed Cade Hawkins loved her.

Quickly, while the image was still in her mind, she grabbed a sketch pad and did another illustration of the dressing-gown evening jacket that had been a part of her portfolio. She would do a masculine variation for J.J.; a well-cut jacket that would make him look sleek and sexy for the amazing woman he'd married.

Tucking the sketchbook under her arm and grabbing the costume she'd almost finished, she left the apartment.

As she drove home she wondered if Cade liked to go dancing. She felt like dancing. When she was happy she always felt like dancing.

Cade's car was in the drive when she pulled up and her heart leaped. It was crazy, she knew, that at twenty-one she was as giddy as a schoolgirl over the sight of a man's car.

But she was.

She opened her trunk when she got out of the car, stashing the sketch pad and costume there. One was a surprise for J.J., the other a surprise for Cade. Both were for later. Both needed work.

"Cade," she yelled out when she entered the house, tossing her keys down on the counter.

No response.

"Shadow . . . ?"

Nothing.

She looked out the living room window into the backyard but it was empty. The house echoed with emptiness, her voice bouncing back to her ears when she called them again, "Cade, Sha-dow?"

And then she saw the note on the refrigerator door, stuck there with a magnet for an auto body shop.

Ashleigh—
Took Shadow for a run.

C

So much for going dancing. Cade would be beat after a day of work and the usual five-mile run with Shadow.

Still too keyed up to relax, Ashleigh decided to change into her leotard and ballet shoes and dance.

She did some freestyle dancing to the CD Cade had on the stereo—The Fabulous Thunderbirds—losing herself in the music.

When the song ended, she heard clapping and turned toward the sound.

It wasn't Cade.

And the clapping wasn't appreciative.

The single, slow beat of the clap was sarcastic.

And chilling.

12

"CAN I HELP YOU?" Ashleigh asked, remaining where she was in the living room.

"It's too late. You wouldn't listen. I tried to get you to listen." Hysteria edged Melodie Fortune's voice.

"Has something happened to Cade!" Ashleigh demanded, catching the hysteria momentarily.

"No."

"I don't understand, Melodie."

"Sure, you do."

"Why don't you tell me?" Ashleigh wondered frantically how long Cade had been gone with Shadow, desperately trying not to panic at the maniacal look in Melodie Fortune's eyes.

"You think you're really pretty, don't you? That you can dance naked and make men do whatever you want them to for you—"

"But I don't dance anymore. You must know that. I'm not working at Miss Olivia's."

"So Cathy said."

"It's true."

"It doesn't matter anymore."

"Look, I'm hot and sweaty from working out. Why don't I get us both a cool drink and we can sit down and talk about what's bothering you," Ashleigh offered, stalling for precious time.

"No. I want you to stay right where you are. You aren't going anywhere, so don't get any cute ideas. Your luck has just run out. Oh, you may be able to fool Cade Hawkins and the others, but you don't fool me for a second. I know what kind of woman you are."

"You do?"

Where was Cade! *Oh, please, come back quick, Cade,* Ashleigh silently prayed.

"Yes, I do. You're the kind of woman who steals other women's men. Don't play innocent with me. It won't work. I know you seduce men away with your wicked dancing."

"But I haven't— What are you talking about?" Ashleigh asked, again trying reason and all the while knowing that it wouldn't work. She knew a fanatical look when she saw one.

She was in danger.

Life-threatening danger.

Please, Cade, come back, she kept thinking, as if thinking could make it happen. She held on, trying not to panic at the thought that he might be too late.

"Maybe this will change things and everything won't come to you so easily when you aren't so pretty any longer, Ashleigh."

Ashleigh gasped when she saw the flash of steel, the long blade of the kitchen knife that had been lying on the kitchen counter. Cade had left it there after slicing an orange in half before he'd gone for his run with Shadow. The two cupped orange peels were still on the countertop when she'd laid her keys beside them.

"I have your keys, too. So don't think about running, because you won't get far. Just stay right here and take what you have coming to you."

"Please, don't do this," Ashleigh begged.

"But I want to."

"You *can't* do this," Ashleigh pleaded, keeping her eye on the shiny knife blade as it waved wildly in the air in a taunting fashion.

"You're wrong. I can do whatever I want. I'm the one in control here. I'm entitled. You need to be punished. If I want to destroy your pretty face, I can. And guess what—I want to."

Ashleigh shifted a little to her left, very slowly, trying to avoid her movement being detected.

"I said, stay where you are. You don't listen very well, do you? But then we already know that, don't we? You didn't pay attention to the threats I made."

Ashleigh remained still, not moving, trying not to agitate Melodie further.

Continuing to play for time, Ashleigh asked, "Is this about me or about Cade?"

"Cade is mine, not yours. When we made love I felt like I might explode, it was that intense because of his strong feelings for me. He is the one person who makes me feel fulfilled. He gave me the passion I've been dreaming of. And you're not going to spoil it. He doesn't love you.

"He loves *me*."

"*You* made love to Cade?"

"Does it surprise you that we are lovers? I don't know why. He even recommended me to Cathy when she needed a lawyer to ditch that jerkface husband of hers. He's only protecting you because you've played on his sympathies. Why, you're pathetic. Cade wants a strong woman like me, not a wimp like you."

"You're lying." Ashleigh couldn't believe Cade and Melodie Fortune had been lovers. Were lovers.

"Do you want me to tell you what he likes? Because I will. I'll tell you—"

Ashleigh put her hands over her ears. "No! I don't want to hear your lies."

Melodie continued torturing her. "I'll tell you how he touched me, how he drove me crazy."

Something had driven the woman crazy, Ashleigh knew. But she couldn't believe it was Cade's touch.

"Then the two of you have been together for a long time . . . ?" Ashleigh asked, her belief in Cade starting to waver. Maybe she'd read more into her relationship with Cade than was there. Perhaps Melodie was right and Cade only felt sorry for her; that he was protecting her as part of his job, and the lovemaking meant nothing to him.

"It doesn't matter how long we've been together," Melodie retorted. "One night of passion like that is all it takes to know when something is as spectacular as what we have together. I know he's sleeping with you, but it doesn't mean anything. Men are weak. I'm the one he really cares about, not you."

And then Ashleigh remembered Monica telling her Cade loved her and knew what she and Cade had wasn't all in her mind. It was real. As real as the knife in Melodie's hand.

"But you're stalling, aren't you?" the other woman sneered. "Hoping Cade will come back and save you. He won't. He doesn't care about you. He told me so when he was making love to me before he left to go run with that stupid dog of his." Melodie started toward Ashleigh, wildly brandishing the knife in front of her.

Her eyes were crazy.

Ashleigh knew she had to save herself.

They both heard the dog bark at the same time.

"It's not them," Melodie said, tossing her dark hair as if to shake off the possibility. Nonetheless she'd stopped to listen.

But the bark didn't sound again.

The front door opened and Cade came inside, calling out Ashleigh's name.

Ashleigh screamed just as Melodie lunged for her, grabbing Ashleigh around the neck and pulling her back against her.

"Don't say a word," Melodie warned, her strength surprising Ashleigh.

"Ashleigh!" Cade ran into the kitchen, stopping when he saw Melodie—and the knife she held at Ashleigh's throat.

"Don't worry, I've got her," Melodie said, smiling at Cade. "I'm going to get rid of her for you so you won't have to be bothered with her anymore. When I dispose of her, I'll come back and we can be together again."

"Are you crazy?" Cade demanded, incredulous at Melodie's words.

He looked at Ashleigh and her eyes told him that, yes, Melodie *was* crazy. He wished he hadn't left Shadow in the backyard.

He knew that if he made a move, he'd endanger Ashleigh; Melodie's grip on the knife was so tight that her knuckles were white.

"Come on, Ashleigh, we're leaving now," Melodie said, pulling her backward toward the patio door.

"No!" Cade started forward instinctively, then stopped when he saw the wild look in Melodie's eyes.

Fear accelerated the black dots swimming in front of Ashleigh's eyes until the room began to waver. The backs of her knees turned to jelly and she fainted, slumping in Melodie's grip just when a loud crash boomed. Shards of flying glass sprayed all directions as a hundred pounds of protective German shepherd lunged into the room, distracting Melodie just long enough for Cade to tackle her and get the knife.

Broken glass was everywhere; a piece of it had cut Ashleigh's arm, which hurt like hell when she came to.

Shadow, his own shoulder cuts bleeding badly, was yowling and trying to drag Melodie away from Cade by the ankle.

Melodie thrashed wildly in an effort to escape both Cade and Shadow. But Cade had her firmly in his grip. "Hold her, boy. Good boy, don't let her move, Shadow," Cade urged, getting up and running for his handcuffs, while Shadow growled fiercely.

Cade was back in a flash, and cuffed Melodie, who swore at him.

As he finished by cuffing her to the wooden leg on his leather sofa, he couldn't resist saying, "It's just business, Melodie."

She spat at him.

"I'm going to kill you," she threatened.

"You're going to jail. Know a good attorney, by any chance?" Cade retorted, calling a cruiser on the telephone.

Ashleigh was crooning to Shadow who lay at her feet whimpering while she picked the bits of glass from his fur. The cuts weren't bad; the worst one was on his shoulder, which had taken the brunt of the impact. The dog had instinctively lowered his head when he'd run full tilt and crashed through the picture window to protect them from danger.

"You're a good boy, a very brave doggy, aren't you?" Ashleigh said, hugging Shadow who was eating up the adoration and whimpering for more.

"And you're going to create a monster," Cade said as he joined Ashleigh. "He's going to want to sleep in the middle of the bed all the time."

"He deserves it. He saved my life, didn't you, boy? You're such a brave Shadow."

Shadow barked his agreement as Cade hunkered down beside the two of them.

"Are you okay?" Cade asked, stroking Ashleigh's throat where a red mark showed, the start of a bruise from the pressure of the knife Melodie had held against her.

"Yes. Just jittery and . . . I'm all right."

"I've never been so scared," Cade admitted. "But then I've never had so much to lose. When I thought I'd lose you, I realized I love you, Ashleigh."

"I love you too, Cade," she responded, kissing him and crying.

Shadow barked for attention and they both laughed.

"We love you too, boy," Cade said, petting him.

As sirens sounded in the distance, both of them looked over at the curiously silent Melodie Fortune.

She lay on her side on the floor with her hands cuffed to the sofa leg. The look in her eyes was terrifying, but the words she mumbled were incoherent, making no sense to anyone but her—and perhaps not even to her.

Epilogue

IT HAD BEEN TWO WEEKS since Melodie Fortune's attempt on Ashleigh's life. The newspapers and tabloid shows had had a field day, calling it The Stripper and the Vice Cop.

But things were beginning to settle down.

Cade was back working Homicide and happy.

Shadow was spoiled beyond repair.

And Ashleigh had presented J.J. and Monica with a custom-made suit for Monica and evening jacket for J.J. as a thank-you for the position of junior designer for the Julian Design Group that Monica had secured for Ashleigh.

The future looked bright.

And the evening Ashleigh had planned for Cade was going to erase everything but pleasure from his mind. She'd finished the surprise costume.

It would be her final private performance... unless he wanted an encore.

Cade was in the shower.

He had the weekend off. He'd need the time to recuperate. Sneaking the costume from its hiding place, she began getting dressed. The striptease tonight would be traditional, with her ending up naked.

Cade could take it from there.

She planned to push every button on his stimulus-response meter, indulging herself in stripping for him alone—which in her mind was what she'd been doing at Miss Olivia's.

When the shower stopped running, Ashleigh turned out the lights and began lighting the candles. Shadow lay by the bed munching on a chew toy she'd given him. Ashleigh had tried coaxing him from the room, but he wouldn't leave her side. Cade had laughingly threatened to sue Ashleigh for alienation of affection.

"Why is it so dark in here? Oh—!" Cade exclaimed, coming from the shower and seeing her bending over the little tray she'd set on the nightstand beside the bed. On the tray were adhesive tape and gauze. Ashleigh wore nurse's whites.

She straightened, adjusting the little white nurse's cap on her head. "I thought I'd change the bandage on your thumb, sir."

Cade's flashy grin made an appearance as he dropped the towel he'd slung around his waist. "By all means . . . nurse."

"If you'll just lie down, sir." She pointed to the bed.

"You will be gentle, won't you?"

"That's up to you. It depends on how much trouble you give me."

Cade caressed the inside of her thigh above the white stocking. "Do men usually give you trouble, nurse?"

She slapped his hand away. One of the things that most fascinated Ashleigh about Cade was that he had a hot body and a cool mind. She planned to seduce his mind first; his body would be putty—or not quite, she thought with a smile.

"*You* aren't going to give me any trouble, are you? You're going to do exactly as I tell you," she ordered, her tone severe.

"Yes, nurse." He was winning the seduction. He already had her distracted by his damned flashy smile. Concentrate, she had to concentrate.

"Now give me your hand," she said, sitting down on the edge of the bed.

"Now we're talking." Cade offered his hand while staring at the cleavage displayed by the undone buttons and a push-up bra. A white lacy push-up bra.

Ashleigh picked up a pair of scissors.

"Wait a minute, be careful with those," Cade said, using his other hand to protect himself—if only partly. After all, he was *really* enjoying the show.

Ashleigh concentrated on cutting through the bandage on Cade's thumb, removing the tape and gauze.

Then she reached for the fresh gauze on the night table but purposely dropped it. It rolled across the floor. "Oh, dear," she cried, getting up. Walking across the floor in her high-heeled white pumps—admittedly not nurse's shoes—she bent low from the waist to retrieve the roll of gauze.

The white uniform she wore was short to begin with. Her bending made it rise above her stocking tops. The white seams on the backs of her white stockings were like arrows pointing to her white silk panties. Ever so slowly she straightened, tugging down the hem of her uniform with false modesty.

"You know, I'm feeling a little weak," Cade said, his eyes twinkling. "I think I could use a little oxygen. You wouldn't be able to spare me some, would you?"

"If you behave," she promised, returning to his side and bending low to kiss him, her teeth first biting at his lips, teasing him, before giving him the seductive kiss he'd been angling for.

When she came up for air, Cade looked a little pale.

"Ah, I don't think that worked. I feel weaker—" he managed.

"Perhaps it was too much for you. Maybe we need to start with less."

"No. I'm feeling better now," he said. "More oxygen, please."

"No, I think you need to wait a bit first. I'll bandage your thumb and then we'll see how you're feeling." Ashleigh wrapped the pristine white gauze around his thumb until she reached the end of the strip she'd cut.

"Hold it, please."

Cade cupped her breast through the snug-fitting nurse's uniform, rubbing his thumb over it provocatively and grinning.

She looked down at his hand and then back up at him, pointedly waiting.

"Oh. Oh, you mean hold the gauze for you," he said, looking innocent, or trying to.

"I still have the scissors," she warned, waving them in the air.

Cade removed his hand and held the end of the gauze strip in place on his injured thumb.

Ashleigh picked up the roll of adhesive tape and cut a short length of it. Applying it to the gauze on Cade's thumb, she wound it around and around until the bandage was secure.

"You did a great job, nurse. It didn't hurt one little bit."

"Thank you." Ashleigh placed the gauze and adhesive back in their respective packages. "Now, is there anything else I can do for you?"

"Since you asked, maybe you could fluff my pillow. I'm feeling a bit uncomfortable. I just can't seem to relax, you know?"

"Fluff your pillow?"

He nodded.

She leaned forward, almost falling out of her uniform as she plumped the pillows behind Cade's head until he was satisfied with her efforts.

"Anything else?" she asked then.

"You know, I'm getting a little chilly," Cade said, rubbing his hands together. "Can you turn up the heat a bit in here?"

Ashleigh considered him. "I only do that for my very favorite patients. The ones who promise to be very, very good," she replied, running her forefinger down his chest until it reached his concave belly.

Cade held up two fingers in a Boy Scout pledge, swearing, "I promise, nurse. I'll be really, really good. The best," he bragged.

She pushed a CD into the portable player she'd placed on the night table and hit Play. A mellow, bluesy saxophone began wailing sexily into the room.

Ashleigh began to move in time to the music. Swaying her hips suggestively, toying with the buttons still fastened on the bodice of the formfitting white uniform.

"Say please," she coaxed.

Cade put his hands together and begged, "Pu-lease."

Ashleigh tried, but just couldn't seem to get the buttons undone. "Maybe you could undo them..." she suggested, moving to the bed.

"Excellent idea." His forehead nuzzled her cleavage as he finished the last button. He began nibbling his way back up to her lips.

She batted her eyelashes at him. "You know, I think it is getting warm in here. Maybe I should take this uniform off. It's just the two of us. You won't tell anyone, will you?"

"Take it off," he agreed. "And I promise it will be our little secret. You are my private nurse, after all, aren't you?" he said, chewing on her earlobe.

Ashleigh got up from the bed and walked away, inching up the short skirt of the uniform, teasing.

"Turn around," he ordered.

She turned.

"Take it off. Now."

"But—" She pretended to have second thoughts.

"I said—do you want me to have to report you?—take it off."

Lifting her chin in mock indignation, she began following his order, slipping the skimpy white uniform off with a shrug and standing before him in her lacy white push-up bra, flirty white silk panties, thigh-high white stockings and matching pumps.

The tables had turned. Cade had seized control of the fantasy.

"Take off the nurse's cap, shake down your hair.... Yeah, like that. Now put the nurse's cap back on. Make sure you fasten it well, because you're not taking it off until morning when you go off duty, nurse. You've been teasing me long enough. Taking advantage of my weakened condition. Now it's time for you to give me the special attention I want."

"Yes, sir. Please don't report me for neglecting you, sir."

"I'll think about it. Maybe, if you please me. Step out of your panties and throw them over here to me."

She did as he asked, watching him, hypnotized.

He caught them one-handed and tucked them beneath his pillow. "A souvenir," he bragged, daring her to object.

She didn't.

"What...what do you want with me?" It was her turn to pretend innocence, but strangely her knees felt like they'd turned to jelly.

His dark eyebrow arched, suggesting amusement.

At that, she wrested back control of the fantasy, turning around and undoing the push-up bra, letting it slip to the floor.

The CD had stopped and the room was silent, the only sound their breathing. Still facing away from him she shook out her hair, letting it flirt with her bare back, inviting his touch.

Then she turned, cupping her breasts in her hands, shielding them as she walked toward him. Stopping beside the bed, she stepped out of her pumps, kicking them aside.

"You did promise to be really, really good," she reminded.

"That I did," Cade said, replacing her hands with his.

She removed his hands. "I'll get the lotion."

"What?"

"For your back rub. We have to give all the patients a back rub before they go to sleep at night."

Cade laughed. "To tell you the truth, I wasn't planning on doing much sleeping. And if I tried to roll over on my stomach right now, I'd break off something you might want to rub later—"

"You mean this . . . ?"

Cade gasped a quick intake of breath when she folded her hand around him.

"Does that feel good?" she asked.

He placed his hands behind his head and pretended to consider her question.

She increased the pressure of her hand, moving it back and forth.

"Uh . . . too good, I think." He reached for her.

He pulled her onto the bed and she straddled him, her hands on his shoulders while he kissed her navel and then lower still. He held her buttocks, squeezing them as she squealed with delight.

"Let me taste you, baby," he urged as she arched backward, resting her elbows on the bed. His tongue made a broad swath—teasing, exciting her until he relented, furling his tongue and thrusting it between the petals of her sex, searching out the tight bud of her desire.

Kissing and nipping, then sucking, he was an abandoned lover, passionate and wild, until he heard her sweet moans of pleasure as she yielded her secrets to him.

And cried out his name again and again.

Her eyes were soft, unfocused, when he pulled her back into his arms. She tasted herself on his lips, tasted his excitement as their lovemaking began in earnest. Her hands were restless in their exploration of his sinewy body. He stilled her hands by enveloping them with his own, his lips going where they would, kissing, licking, sucking until she was mindless with need for him.

He pulled her beneath him. "Tell me," he whispered hoarsely.

"You're very, very good."

"No, tell me you love me."

"I love you, sir."

"And promise me you'll always be my very own private nurse. Promise you'll never leave me."

"I'll never leave you, sir," she promised, raking her nails down his back.

"And that you'll always take such good care of me, even when I'm bad . . ."

"Especially when you're bad— Please, sir," she begged as he withheld what she arched for.

"Tell me...."

"I'll take— Sir!"

"Is that a complaint, nurse?"

"Oh, no, sir."

"And my name is ... ?"

"Mr. Mel Gibson ..."

"No!" He thrust home his point.

"Oh, Mr. Tom Cruise ..."

"No!" He thrust home his point.

"Oh, I remember, Mr. Lucky Vanous ..."

"No!" He thrust home his point.

"I know. Mr. Brad Pitt ..."

"No-o-o!" He stopped thrusting and she stopped laughing.

"Mr. Cade Hawkins, sir," she supplied immediately, encouraging him to continue what he'd so rudely interrupted just as—

"Nurse ..." he groaned, his body slick with sweat.

"Wha-a-at?" Ashleigh moaned, breathy with passion from his delicious lovemaking.

"You give good medicine."

"Thank you, sir."

"You're welcome.... Oh, baby, o-o-ohh ..."

J.J. STOOD AT THE ALTAR, waiting, and looking resplendent in his black double-breasted shawl-collar tuxedo. He was relieved the cummerbund and bow tie Monica had selected wasn't going to get him any ribbing from the churchful of cops making up the guests at the wedding. He'd never been a best man before—except Monica kept informing him he'd been the best man at their wedding.

The wedding—with eight bridesmaids in a Baptist church, with a cake-and-punch reception—had been the first thing Monica had talked him into. The latest was the picture he carried in his wallet— a sonogram of a baby boy.

J.J. straightened the boutonniere on his lapel and winked at Cade as the wedding march began and they turned their attention to Monica who had begun her walk down the center aisle of the church as matron of honor to Ashleigh.

The small bouquet of pastel roses in her hand shook. J.J. knew she was a little unsteady after having just tossed her cookies. Morning sickness was not her idea of a pretty pregnancy and she complained loudly and often to him. But he knew it was all going to be worth it. They had both cried when they'd seen the sonogram.

He hadn't wanted a baby. Working the mean streets of the city, he saw too much of the worst the world had to offer. But when he'd seen his unborn child, their child, he'd seen the best the world had to offer—hope.

They were already arguing—little spats, really, that were excuses for making up in bed afterward—over how she was going to dress their son. J.J. insisted absolutely no short pants and sissy shoes.

He expected he was wasting his breath. He hadn't exactly been a fashion plate when they'd met. Monica had turned him into a secret peacock. While he groused about the way she dressed him, he would never have allowed it if he didn't secretly enjoy it.

J.J. winked at her as she took her place at the altar across from him and Cade.

Cade was all flashy smile—and butterfly stomach, J.J. would bet. He looked happy. And nervous as hell.

Cade wanted to see Ashleigh.

She'd insisted it was bad luck for him to see her the night before the wedding, so she'd stayed with Monica and J.J. and come with them to the church.

J.J. kept assuring Cade that she was there.

Still, he was nervous. He wouldn't be happy until he had Ashleigh on his arm. There was still time for her to change her mind. To take the job in New

York she'd been offered as a designer. Ashleigh had told him what she really wanted was to open her own boutique, with one-of-a-kind designs. With the Internet, faxes, and so on, it was possible to live outside New York and Los Angeles and still be involved in the fashion business.

She'd convinced him it was true, but she was still giving up a lot to be with him. He'd offered to relocate in New York. A cop could work anywhere—it was probably the job with the most security of all. Crime was not taking a holiday in the nineties.

But Ashleigh had insisted she was happy and could fulfill all her dreams just where she was. He wanted to believe her.

She'd even learned to watch Monday-night football and he'd learned to watch "Style" on CNN. Heck, the runway shows featuring scantily-clad models weren't much different than Miss Olivia's.

As Ashleigh put it, they'd done a double rescue.

He'd been afraid he was unlovable, and had acted that way. She'd insisted she loved him, and that he wanted to be loved; which was why he needed to rescue everyone.

She didn't like his being a cop; didn't like the danger or the threat it was to marriage. But she wasn't willing to close herself off to love just to close herself off from pain. If J.J. and Monica could make it work and be happy, then so could they, she'd promised him.

And he'd promised he wouldn't overprotect her. That she could be as independent as she wanted— as long as she loved him.

The debt her ex-husband had saddled her with had almost caused their breakup. They'd argued and argued about it. She didn't want to burden Cade with it. She'd wanted to wait until she'd paid it off.

But in the end Cade had convinced her to see things his way. He didn't want to wait. He'd waited long enough for love. Teasingly he'd bartered that he'd pay off the debt and she could repay him with private performances—she could "nurse" him back to health all she wanted, and cheer him on, and feather-dust him and read to him the library books that were kept under lock and key....

The wedding march began and Cade gave a sigh of relief when he saw his bride appear at the back of the church with her father. It was amazing how he didn't need her touch to set him afire. Just the look of her.

And she was marrying him.

Ashleigh had designed and sewn her wedding dress herself . . . had even hidden a lucky charm in the hem. The dress was hand-finished inside and out, and it fit her to perfection. Subtly sophisticated, the dress had a flawless simplicity. The ivory linen bodice led to a sheer organza overskirt with a long organdy sash at the waist.

Ashleigh saw Cade's eyes smile when she neared and he noticed her headpiece and veil. She wore a tiny hat with pearl beading and a tuft of pleated white tulle that made it vaguely reminiscent of a nurse's cap.

Ashleigh stumbled briefly at the look of love in Cade's eyes, catching her white damask lace-up boot on the decorative runner lining the center aisle of the church. Looking down for a moment she saw the rose petals scattered at her feet by one of Allen's and Brown's nieces, who'd served as flower girl.

The rose petals reminded Ashleigh of another time of rose petals beneath her.... When she looked back up at Cade, she was indeed a blushing bride.

She left her father's arm when he gave her away to Cade. Standing beside him, she pledged her love.

A love she hadn't known she could feel.

And once they'd retrieved the ring a nervous J.J. had dropped, they exchanged rings and were pronounced husband and wife. "Mr. and Mrs. Cade Hawkins."

"DO YOU THINK ANYONE suspects?" Ashleigh asked, as Cade nuzzled her ear, nearly undoing the pearl ear stud that matched her headpiece trim.

"Nope."

"What about Shadow?"

"Nope."

"Then we're safe."

"We're safe," Cade assured her, reaching for the champagne the Ritz Carlton had provided with the honeymoon suite they'd rented for the entire week. After looking through brochures for the Caribbean, Hawaii and Mexico, they'd decided to hide out at the Ritz—without the stress and bother of travel. There had been a lot of changes in their lives in a short amount of time and what both of them wanted was just some down time alone. Later there'd be vacations and travel, but for now all they wanted was each other.

Cade poured the bubbling champagne into the crystal goblets and handed her one. Taking the other, he proposed a toast. "For all the days of our lives . . ." he began.

"And the nights . . ." she interrupted, giggling at the bubbles that tickled her nose as she drank.

"Speaking of which," Cade said, reaching for the oblong box tied with white ribbon in his suitcase, "this is for you. It's something I noticed you didn't have."

Ashleigh lifted the lid of the box and squealed, "You shouldn't have!"

"I had to," Cade replied, watching her lift the silver stethoscope from the gift box. "You'll need it to make sure I'm still breathing in the morning."

"So you think you'll last till morning—"

"If I don't I'll die happy." Cade shrugged, unconcerned, as she placed the stethoscope back in the box and went to retrieve his gift from her suitcase.

"And this is something I noticed you didn't have," Ashleigh said with a secret smile as she handed Cade the square beribboned box.

"PSL tickets for the Rams?" he said hopefully.

"I'm bankrupt, so if I were you I wouldn't count on it."

"Guess we'll all just have to continue watching the games at The Dry Dock on TV." Cade untied the ribbon and opened the box.

"What is this?" he asked, puzzled, lifting the item from the box and holding it up.

"It's a new holster for your gun."

"Huh?" Cade stared at the scrap of heavy fabric with elastic straps. "It looks like a jockstrap!"

"That's what I said. It's a Kevlar jockstrap I custom made for you. I mean, you have a bulletproof vest and yet you let the most valuable thing on your body hang out there all unprotected. Wait till you wear it. All the other cops are going to want one," Ashleigh said, giggling.

"All the other cops are *not* going to know about this. Do you hear me, Ashleigh? Especially J.J."

"If you say so," she agreed reluctantly.

"I say so." He tried to suppress a grin as he dropped the thing back in the box and set it in his suitcase.

"I'm going to order us a late-night snack," he said, changing the subject as he picked up the phone. "Is there anything special you want from room service?"

"Surprise me," she said, untying his tuxedo tie and starting to unbutton his tuxedo shirt as he ordered.

She was so good at distracting him that he had to give his order twice to get it right.

"Strawberries in October?" Ashleigh said when he hung up the phone.

"Strawberries *and* whipped cream. I thought it would be too obvious, just ordering the whipped cream, Mrs. Hawkins. I do have your reputation to think of now that you're going to be designing for the most stylish members of the community."

"You, Mr. Hawkins, are incorrigible."

"Umm . . ." he murmured, untying the long organdy sash at her waist. "That is why you like me, isn't it, Mrs. Hawkins?"

"Who said anything about liking you?" Ashleigh teased, her hands shoving off his tuxedo jacket. "I married you for your money."

That got a laugh. "Apparently no one has told you what cops earn. . . ."

Ashleigh finished undoing the buttons on Cade's tuxedo shirt and pushed it open, letting her hands travel over the warmth of his honed chest. "Oh, well. Then I guess I'll just have to make the best of it."

"You don't want to have the marriage annulled?" he asked, taking her hand and licking her palm, his eyes drinking in hers.

"Actually, I'm planning to make sure tonight makes an annulment impossible."

"Gonna try out the new stethoscope, huh?" He chuckled, sucking her fingers.

"Don't worry, I'll 'nurse' you back to health."

There was a knock on the door, interrupting their love play.

Cade went to answer it, taking their order from room service and tipping heavily, anxious to get back to his bride.

"You were saying…" Cade continued, setting the strawberries and whipped cream on the night table by the bed, and returning to her side. He began fumbling with the row of tiny satin-covered buttons that ran down the back of her gown.

"This may take a while," she said, marking his progress to the second button. "Bring me a couple of strawberries to give me strength."

He snagged two berries and fed them to her seductively, then anxiously resumed the task of getting her out of her dress.

"Why did you put on so many of these damn little buttons? Haven't you heard they've invented the zipper?" Cade grumbled.

"Buttons are prettier, and besides, undoing them all builds sexual tension."

"I don't think we need any help with sexual tension, do you?" he asked, biting her neck. "And by the way, I owe you a hickey in a prominent spot. I don't think the guys are ever going to let me live *that* down."

"They noticed it, huh?" Ashleigh said, giggling.

"After J.J. pointed it out over the address system, they did.

"There, that's the last one," Cade announced, ecstatic over the completion of his mission. "There aren't any other booby traps, are there?"

"Nope, I'm braless—"

"I'm so glad I didn't know that till now. I'd never had made it through the ceremony," he vowed. Eagerly helping her slip out of the dress, he carefully laid it over the love seat across from the bed.

"Take off your shirt," Ashleigh ordered, standing before him topless when he turned. "I'm feeling a little underdressed."

She didn't have to repeat her request.

Her satin tap pants had garters attached, holding up the sheer white stockings.

"I think I know what to do about that," Cade promised, pulling his belt free and slipping it from his narrow waist. Unzipping his pants, he sat down and removed his shoes and socks.

When he stepped out of his trousers, he was naked and proud as he went to retrieve the bowl of whipped cream. Back at Ashleigh's side, he dipped his fingers in the whipped cream, then dabbed the peaks of her bare breasts with the creamy white dollops.

He stood back a moment then, studying her, his flashy grin spreading all the way to his eyes.

"What . . . ?" she demanded.

"I was just thinking, bride," he said, licking the whipped cream from his fingertips with sexual suggestion, "that you look excellent in white."

HARLEQUIN® Temptation

Secret Fantasies

Do you have a secret fantasy?

Kasey Halliday does—she's fallen hard for the "boy" next door. Will Eastman is sexy, sophisticated and definitely interested in Kasey. But there's a mysterious side to this man she can't quite fathom. Find out what Will is hiding in #554 STRANGER IN MY ARMS by Madeline Harper—available in September 1995.

Everybody has a secret fantasy. And you'll find them all in Temptation's exciting new yearlong miniseries, Secret Fantasies. Beginning January 1995, one book each month focuses on the hero's or heroine's innermost romantic desires....

MILLION DOLLAR SWEEPSTAKES (III)

MOVE OVER, MELROSE PLACE!

Apartment for rent
One bedroom
Bachelor Arms
555-1234

Come live and love in L.A. with the tenants of Bachelor Arms. Enjoy a year's worth of wonderful love stories and meet colorful neighbors you'll bump into again and again.

Startling events from Bachelor Arms' past return to stir up scandal, heartache and painful memories for three of its tenants. Read popular Candace Schuler's three sexy and exciting books to find out how passion, love and betrayal at Bachelor Arms affect the lives of three dynamic men. Bestselling author of over fifteen romance novels, Candace is sure to keep you hooked on Bachelor Arms with her steamy, sensual stories.

LOVERS AND STRANGERS #549 (August 1995)

SEDUCED AND BETRAYED #553 (September 1995)

PASSION AND SCANDAL #557 (October 1995)

Next to move into Bachelor Arms are the heroes and heroines in books by ever-popular Judith Arnold!

Don't miss the goings-on at Bachelor Arms

Can an invitation to a bachelor
auction, be the beginning
of true love?

Find out in Tiffany White's sexy,
sassy new book from

▼ SILHOUETTE YOURS TRULY™

MALE FOR SALE

Noelle Perry was dateless in Chicago. Her sister's wedding was only days away and she needed to find a man—fast! Friends suggested she attend a bachelor auction and buy herself a conservative businessman in a three-piece suit. Instead, she got a sexy bad boy in a black leather jacket. Surely Hunter Ashton could act like a gentleman, discuss golf with her dad and look at her adoringly. Right? Well, two out of three ain't bad....

Available this September at your favorite retail outlet.

And in September and October, *Yours Truly*™ offers you not one but TWO proofs of purchase toward your Pages & Privileges gifts and benefits!

Love—when you least expect it!

▼ *Silhouette*®

YTTW

URBAN COWBOYS

A Stetson and spurs don't make a man a cowboy.

Being a real cowboy means being able to tough it out on the ranch and on the range. Three Manhattan city slickers with something to prove meet that challenge…and succeed.

But are they man enough to handle the three wild western women who lasso their hearts?

Bestselling author Vicki Lewis Thompson will take you on the most exciting trail ride of your life with her fabulous new trilogy— Urban Cowboys.

THE TRAILBLAZER #555 (September 1995)

THE DRIFTER #559 (October 1995)

THE LAWMAN #563 (November 1995)

HARLEQUIN® *Temptation*®

UC-G

RUGGED. SEXY. HEROIC.

OUTLAWS *and* HEROES

Stony Carlton—A lone wolf determined never to be tied down.

Gabriel Taylor—Accused and found guilty by small-town gossip.

Clay Barker—At Revenge Unlimited, he *is* the law.

JOAN JOHNSTON, DALLAS SCHULZE and MALLORY RUSH, three of romance fiction's biggest names, have created three unforgettable men—modern heroes who have the courage to fight for what is right....

OUTLAWS AND HEROES—available in September wherever Harlequin books are sold.

 HARLEQUIN ®

OUTH

As a *Privileged Woman,*
you'll be entitled to all
these *Free Benefits.*
And *Free Gifts,* too.

To thank you for buying our books, we've designed an exclusive FREE program called *PAGES & PRIVILEGES*™. You can enroll with just one Proof of Purchase, and get the kind of luxuries that, until now, you could only read about.

*B*IG HOTEL DISCOUNTS

A privileged woman stays in the finest hotels. And so can you—at up to 60% off! Imagine standing in a hotel check-in line and watching as the guest in front of you pays $150 for the same room that's only costing you $60. Your *Pages & Privileges* discounts are good at Sheraton, Marriott, Best Western, Hyatt and thousands of other fine hotels all over the U.S., Canada and Europe.

*F*REE DISCOUNT TRAVEL SERVICE

A privileged woman is always jetting to romantic places. When <u>you</u> fly, just make one phone call for the lowest published airfare at time of booking—<u>or double the difference back!</u> PLUS— you'll get a $25 voucher to use the first time you book a flight AND <u>5% cash back on every ticket you buy thereafter through the travel service!</u>

HT-PP4A

$\mathcal{F}$REE GIFTS!

A privileged woman is always getting wonderful gifts.
Luxuriate in rich fragrances that will stir your senses (and his). This gift-boxed assortment of fine perfumes includes three popular scents, each in a beautiful designer bottle. Truly Lace...This luxurious fragrance unveils your sensuous side.

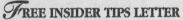

L'Effleur...discover the romance of the Victorian era with this soft floral. Muguet des bois...a single note floral of singular beauty.

YOURS FREE!

$50 VALUE

$\mathcal{F}$REE INSIDER TIPS LETTER

A privileged woman is always informed. And you'll be, too, with our free letter full of fascinating information and sneak previews of upcoming books.

$\mathcal{M}$ORE GREAT GIFTS & BENEFITS TO COME

A privileged woman always has a lot to look forward to. And so will you. You get all these wonderful FREE gifts and benefits now with only one purchase...and there are no additional purchases required. However, each additional retail purchase of Harlequin and Silhouette books brings you a step closer to even more great FREE benefits like half-price movie tickets... and even more FREE gifts.

L'Effleur...This basketful of romance lets you discover L'Effleur from head to toe, heart to home.

Truly Lace...
A basket spun with the sensuous luxuries of Truly Lace, including Dusting Powder in a reusable satin and lace covered box.

Complete the Enrollment Form in the front of this book and mail it with this Proof of Purchase.